He had buns that put Mel Gibson's to shame.

Lucky blinked but he didn't disappear. *They* didn't disappear. Tight, tanned, muscular and curved just so... She couldn't help but wonder what kind of workout would yield such spectacular results. Undoubtedly a rigorous one, with lots of flexing, pumping, grinding...

Reason kicked in and she inched backward into the shelter of the trees. She had to get out of there before he caught sight of her. But then the man scooped up several handfuls of water, doused them onto his body, and Lucky lost what little common sense she had. The muscles in his arms rippled, catching gleaming rays of sunlight. Water streamed over his shoulders, down the curve of his back and those spectacular buns.

Lucky wiped at a trickle of sweat. Thank God she'd brought an extra package of chewing gum or her throat would be sandpaper—

Pop!

The bubble burst. And Tight Tush jerked around. Lucky threw away her gum disgustedly. How could she have forgotten about it? She clamped her eyes shut and held her breath. Maybe she'd be lucky. Maybe he hadn't seen her. Lord knew she was due....

She heard a deep, rich voice drawl, *"Enjoying the view?"*

Dear Reader,

Our heroines come in all kinds of shapes and sizes with the differing personalities to match, but one common trait is their reaction to that unexpected delivery...children! We have two very fun and different stories this month about a mom-to-be and an apprentice nanny.

In *Regarding Rita* by Gwen Pemberton, the entire town of teeny Hooperville is involved in waitress Rita Lynn's pregnancy—and in the hunt for a suitable daddy candidate. Poor ex-city slicker Nate Morrow has no idea what's about to hit him! Moreover the last thing the former divorce attorney wants is to marry, but the good folks of Hooperville have decided a wedding is just what they—and Rita Lynn—need.

Cowboy Tyler Grant needs a nanny real fast, so when Lucky Myers walks through his door to return his lost wallet he decides he's found the right woman to look after his daughter temporarily. Wrong! Lucky is all heart, but she's not much of a lady—which is what his ex-mother-in-law's family expects. So Tyler ends up playing Henry Higgins to his own Eliza Doolittle, with the expected results...and ends up *Gettin' Lucky*.

Enjoy our stories.

With love and laughter,

Malle Vallik

Malle Vallik
Associate Senior Editor

GETTIN' LUCKY
Kimberly Raye

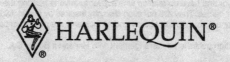

HARLEQUIN®

TORONTO • NEW YORK • LONDON
AMSTERDAM • PARIS • SYDNEY • HAMBURG
STOCKHOLM • ATHENS • TOKYO • MILAN • MADRID
PRAGUE • WARSAW • BUDAPEST • AUCKLAND

ISBN 0-373-44050-2

GETTIN' LUCKY

If it weren't for bad luck, I'd have no luck at all....

Like my heroine Lucky, I've never been very lucky myself. Always a day late and a dollar short. No breasts out to here, or legs up to there, or tall, dark strangers beating down my door (except for the UPS guy, of course, but he charges me so I don't think he counts).

Forever the optimist, however, I'm a firm believer that Lady Luck shines on even the unluckiest at least once. Sometimes twice, and I have a loving husband and rowdy toddler to prove it. (Okay, so maybe the toddler came from Lady You-don't-know-what-real-work-is-until-you're-crawling-around-under-a-highchair-chasing-runaway-peas, but hey, I'm an optimist.) So keep smiling and hoping, and if She hasn't graced you with a smile yet, She will, at least once or twice. Make that three times—Hark! I think I hear the UPS hunk—er, man knocking right now!

—Kimberly Raye

For my mother,
Estella Adams, who gave birth to me,
raised me and most of all loved me.
Thanks, Ma!

And for my editor, Brenda Chin.
For her hard work, dedication and patience.
You're the best!

1

FOR CABDRIVER Lucky Myers, the only thing worse than bursting into tears was doing it smack-dab in the middle of Houston's largest airport. On a busy Friday morning. And on a major PMS day.

"Yo, Lucky!" came the familiar male voice.

And in front of Buster would-you-look-at-the-hooters-on-that-one? Sinclair, fellow cabdriver and male chauvinist extraordinaire.

If it wasn't for bad luck, I'd have no luck at all. She swiped at her eyes and handed the passenger who got out of her cab a travel bag.

"Thanks so much for being understanding," said the woman, dressed in a cherry-red suit. "And for listening." She shoved her suitcases at a nearby baggage clerk. "I just knew I was going to miss my plane, but thanks to you I'll make it!"

A treacherous tear slid from the corner of Lucky's eye and she dashed it away, disgusted with herself. Geez, she could sympathize with the woman, but she didn't have to do it in front of hundreds of travelers. Besides, people had heart attacks every day. Just because the woman's father had suffered a severe one and was, at this moment, hanging on to life by little more than a thread didn't give Lucky any call to act like a blubbering idiot. She hardly knew her, much less the father.

But she knew how the woman felt. Lucky had lost her own father last year. When the passenger had climbed into the back of the cab and poured out her tearful story, Lucky might very well have been hearing her own. Minus the husband and daughter waiting at home in some little rinky-dink Texas town, of course.

She sniffled, struggling for her composure as Buster headed straight for her.

Black hair slicked back à la Elvis, he wore a neon-pink flamingo-print shirt unbuttoned to midchest and a dozen faux gold chains around his neck. Shirttails flapped in the wind, giving an occasional glimpse of the overstuffed waistline of his much-too-tight white jeans.

But the absolute worst thing about Buster, who looked at anything with breasts, was the fact that he never even spared Lucky a glance. Not that she wanted him to, mind you. But it was the principle of the thing. All of her life, male attention had passed her by in favor of better faces, bigger breasts, more shapely rear ends. That bad-luck thing again.

"Hiya, babe," he said, coming up to her. "You just drop off the fare you picked up at the Four Seasons? I bet she tipped out the wazoo. Stella said she was loaded."

Oh no! Lucky shot a watery gaze at her meter box. A sick feeling churned in the pit of her stomach. Forget the tip. The woman hadn't even paid her fare and Lucky had been too worried about helping the poor, distraught thing unload her luggage to notice.

She whirled, blinking furiously as she strained to see through the crowd. She caught a glimpse of a red skirt, red three-inch heels clattering behind a cart of speeding luggage.

"Hey!" she shouted. "Wait!" But the flash of color was gone and so was Lucky's eighty-dollar cab fare.

Eighty dollars. The sick feeling graduated to full-blown nausea. More tears burned her eyes.

"So how much tip—whoa, do my eyes deceive me? Can this be tough-as-nails Lucky Myers *crying?*"

"I'm not crying. It's just allergies."

"You have allergies and moved to Texas? This is the pollen capital of the South..." The words faded when a blonde in a halter top swayed past them. "Wow. Would you look at the hoo—"

"Is that all you ever think of?" Lucky snapped.

"What can I say? I'm a romantic kind of guy." He waggled his bushy black eyebrows, the expression like two caterpillars doing a mating dance.

Lucky couldn't hold back a smile. Buster's outlook on women was so totally clueless, it was hard to keep a straight face, much less stay mad at the guy. "So you skipped all the way across the taxi lane to tell me what a Valentino you are?"

"Actually, no," he said, his hand going to his hip pocket. Due to the extraordinary tightness of his pants it took him a good thirty seconds before the envelope finally squirmed free. "When I checked in for my shift at the cab company, the mailman was there with this letter. Stella asked me to give it to you since I was headed your way. She thought it might be important."

Lucky took the envelope, her attention stuck on the return address: Marshall Nursing Home. She ripped open the seal and read the statement of account. The dread churning in her stomach settled into a hard lump by the time she reached the sum printed at the bottom. Oh no.

"Your grandma?"

"Yeah."

"She's okay, right?"

"She's fine." Lucky folded the letter and slipped it into her pocket. "Everything's fine, as long as I win the lottery."

"That nursing home really eating up your cash?"

"Yeah, but it's worth it." Despite her mood, she managed a smile. "It's got this beautiful flower garden, with roses and daisies. That's why Daddy moved her down here from Chicago." Her eyes burned with a new bout of tears and she blinked. "He managed the expense when he was alive, and so will I. There's still three weeks until the payment is due. I've got nearly two thousand saved for school..." Suddenly the lump in her stomach felt like burning lead. If she drained her

savings, she wouldn't be able to pay her tuition in the spring.
At the rate she was going, she would never finish her teaching
degree.

But her granny was the only family she had left now.

"I can do this," she said, more for herself than Buster.
"With my savings and a few extra shifts on the weekends, I
can make the three thousand."

"Whew!" Buster whistled. "Three thousand. I guess bowling with me and the guys is out tomorrow night then."

"I'm afraid so." Though that in itself was a blessing. Lucky
wasn't in the mood for another Saturday night spent watching
Buster and the guys guzzle beer and ogle women at the Bowl-
A-Rama. She'd started Saturday night bowling in a desperate
effort to beef up her nonexistent social life. How was she
supposed to meet Mr. Perfect if she didn't get out and mingle?
Unfortunately, Mr. Perfect, or even Mr. Almost Perfect, didn't
hang out at the Bowl-A-Rama.

A good man. That's all she wanted out of life. That, her
teaching degree and three thousand dollars. The last two she
could earn, but the man was another story. How could she find
herself a good one when even the not-so-good ones didn't give
her the time of day?

"Geez, babe," Buster went on, "we're bowling against the
Fast Cab Kangaroos and we really need that arm of yours—"
He fell silent when he saw an attractive woman, bags in hand,
standing near his abandoned cab. "Later, babe. I think I'm in
love." He made a beeline for his taxi.

"Lucky?" came the female voice from the CB mounted on
Lucky's dash. "Are you finished at the airport yet? I've got
a fare going from the Hyatt Regency to the convention center."

"I'm on it, Stella," she said into the mike. Then she
climbed into the back seat of her cab and bent to retrieve a
gum wrapper. "Holy Moses," Lucky breathed when she spotted a man's wallet stuffed with a wad of bills. Not fives, or

tens, or even twenties, she quickly discovered. No, there were a few fifties, and the rest were hundreds. Hundreds!

The answer to Lucky's feverish prayers. No more overtime. No more double shifts...

Before she could drop to her knees and thank the powers above, the red-dressed woman's desperate words replayed in her head. *"One minute my poor daddy was fine, and the next, he was at Death's door. I just don't know what I'll do if I lose him."*

The wallet had to belong to the woman. Lucky had a habit of checking the cab after every customer, and she knew it hadn't been there before the stop at the Four Seasons. Sympathy swept through Lucky like a heat wave through Houston. The woman had probably been in such a hurry, she hadn't bothered to transfer the money and credit cards to her own wallet. She'd simply grabbed her husband's and rushed off to be with her father. Now the poor thing had no money, no wallet, nothing. She was destitute. Unless...

Lucky could turn over the wallet to the police and let them make the return. But with her string of rotten luck, it would likely get stuck in a bunch of red tape. No, speed was important. The woman's father was dying. Death didn't wait for the mail, or even Federal Express.

Lucky opened the wallet, her gaze flicking over the dozens of credit cards peeking from the leather slots. Finally she found an ID card with a man's name—undoubtedly the husband's—and an address for their hometown. Locking up her cab, she rushed to a nearby pay phone and dialed Information.

"I'm sorry, but that number is unlisted," the operator said.

"But this is an emergency, a major emergency. You see, one of my customers left her husband's wallet in my cab, and I'm afraid she doesn't have any other money and she's off to see her father who's dying and—"

"Rules are rules. Would you like me to check another number for you?"

"No," Lucky replied. "Thanks, anyway." She slid the receiver into place and walked back to her cab.

She knew what she should do, but that would mean giving up an entire day's worth of work. The nursing-home bill burned through her pocket. *Remember me?* Remember Granny and the three-thousand-dollar flowers? On the other hand, her conscience wouldn't let her forget the woman's frantic voice. "He's dying. My poor daddy's dying."

"Okay," she finally said. She hauled open the door to her cab. "The Lucky Express to the rescue."

Reaching into her own pocket, Lucky counted out eighty dollars and slid the money into the fare box. She'd do the Good Samaritan thing, take the wallet back to the husband, then collect her eighty bucks from him. Better to cover the fare with her own money and wait an extra day than go back and tell Stella and the other cabbies she'd been stiffed.

That would be almost as bad as the crying—

She was *not* crying.

Lucky placed the wallet on the seat next to her, revved the engine and pulled into the flow of traffic. Grabbing the CB mike, she radioed Stella that she was taking the day off, much to the other woman's astonishment. A quick road trip and the wallet predicament would be solved. Then she could concentrate on making the nursing-home money, and go back to hunting for Mr. Perfect.

Of course, she'd have to try a new hunting ground. The Bowl-A-Rama was a complete bust. Maybe she could answer one of those singles ads. Or call one of those dating services. Yeah, those were possibilities. Okay, so maybe they were more like long shots, but a girl had to start somewhere.

HELL. She'd driven straight into the middle of hell.

Only hell could be this hot in October.

Just her luck, she thought, blowing a large bubble with her chewing gum. Lucky had never lived up to her name. Now, if she'd been called *Un*lucky Myers, well, that would have hit the nail right on the head. A flat tire, a broken air conditioner and at least a hundred extra miles she hadn't counted on—all in the past four hours. What a way to kill a Friday afternoon. So much for this trip being simple.

At least it couldn't get any worse, she thought as she blew another bubble. She hefted the tire she'd just changed into the trunk, then leaned against the bumper to catch her breath.

On second thought… The pressure built and she crossed her legs. Blast that six-pack of diet soda! She should have thrown every can back into the cooler when she'd stopped in Ulysses, the last resemblance to a town she'd seen since getting stuck in a maze of back roads. It seemed that Tyler Grant, the name written on the ID card, didn't actually live in Ulysses. The Grant spread was just "a spit and a throw past the Grant County limits," the waitress at Big Bubba's Diner had told her when she'd stopped to ask directions. If only Lucky knew exactly how far "a spit and a throw" was, she'd be in business.

Somebody upstairs was definitely out to get her. First the heat, and now acres and acres of land with no sign of civilization, much less a rest room. Right now, she'd settle for a tree. A quick glance around at the endless stretch of pastureland, and she realized that was about as likely as Brad Pitt beating down her door for a date—*Come on, Brad!* Her gaze fixed on a patch of trees in the distance.

She slammed the trunk closed. "Sorry, baby, but you're on your own for the next few minutes." She stroked the Chevy's hood. Her father had loved this car with a vengeance, and Lucky had loved him, and while he might be gone, there was a part of him still with her. She smiled and patted the Chevy again. "Don't go picking up any men without me." Then she grabbed a few tissues and headed for the white wooden fence lining the road.

Shade! her heated body screamed.

Relief! cried the six-pack yearning to be free.

She walked and sweated. And sweated and walked, until

her cab disappeared behind her and perspiration drenched her T-shirt. Finally, after a good ten minutes dodging her way past cow patties, she reached the blessed shade. Not merely a few trees, she quickly realized, but a full-blown forest. She walked deeper before finding a spot to relieve the drought for a patch of thirsty grass.

Afterward, she turned to head back the way she'd come. Then turned again. And again. Lost. Great. Just *great.*

Her ears perked up when she heard a noise. *Clop-clop…* Desperate, she followed the sound through the maze of trees. Either she found a way out of here, or she'd melt. Like an ice-cream cone in a microwave oven.

Not that she was whining. Okay, so maybe a little. But even old Satan would be confessing his sins in this heat, *if* he found it bearable. Which he wouldn't. It wasn't hell, it was hotter than hell. Yep, the devil would have already bargained his soul and packed a bag for the Poconos.

Then again, she admitted several minutes later as she stared past the branches of an enormous tree, the Poconos were a little overrated. Her attention fixed on the very big, very dangerous-looking man who'd just galloped up to the river on one of the most beautiful horses Lucky had ever seen.

So the devil rode a horse. Well, she *was* in Texas.

TYLER GRANT REINED his mount to a halt, slid to the ground and unzipped his pants. Seconds later, he stood on the isolated riverbank completely naked, and mad as hell.

Damn that woman!

The past twenty-four hours rushed through his head with all the fury of a tornado. Hell, he felt as if he'd been hit by one.

He had. One in the form of an educated, attractive, reputable nanny, who'd turned out to be nothing more than a thieving con artist. He still couldn't believe it. He'd handpicked the woman from a dozen applications provided by the Dalton Agency, one of the most reputable employment agencies in the state, and checked each one of her impeccable references himself. It had all been a lie, he'd been scammed, and now he was in big trouble.

And he always came here when he was in trouble.

The water winked at him, its mirrorlike surface catching rays of sunlight that spilled through the branches of the towering trees sheltering the river. Memories pulled at him of long-ago summers: inner tubes tied to the surrounding trees, excited boys swinging out over the river, plunging into the water...

He stepped into the river. The water embraced his heated, tense body, pulled at his muscles to relax. Despite the past few hours, the never-ending demands of the ranch, the phone calls to the local sheriff about the thieving nanny, he smiled. The water was heaven. Home. God, it had been so long. Too long.

Guilt shot through Tyler and fired his resolve. He was home now, and he was staying, or so he hoped.

He had to find a new nanny, and fast.

His mother-in-law arrived tomorrow and she expected a governess for her granddaughter. If Helen Bell-Whitman didn't find one—one that met her high standards—he knew she'd cause such a ruckus they'd hear her all the way to the next county. His ears still rang from the moment he'd told Helen he was going home, and that was almost two months ago.

"You're going to go play nursemaid for a man who's had simple eye surgery? Hire someone to nurse him, Tyler. His condition is far from life threatening."

"It's not that simple," he'd told her. "Someone has to look after the ranch. Dad'll be out of circulation for at least a couple of months until his eyes heal from the surgery. He just purchased a new stud and somebody has to oversee the breeding."

"Breeding? Tyler, you're a partner in one of the largest private investment firms in the country, for heaven's sake!

You run board meetings, not breeding sessions. Hire someone to handle that revolting work for you.''

"He's my father, Helen.'' And I owe him, he added silently. For all those years I left him alone.

"There's no need to dirty your own hands over some misguided sense of duty. You're an investment banker, not a rancher.''

In another life, he thought. That part of him was dead and buried alongside his late wife. Nan had wanted him to be a banker, just as his own mother had wanted it. He'd given up the ranch for them, for a different world where he'd never fit in.

But this he was doing not only for his father, but also for his daughter, Bernadette. To show her another side of her heritage and see her smile again. And he *liked* getting his hands dirty. Working cattle involved dirt and sweat, calluses and aching muscles, and he'd never felt more alive.

Of course, Helen couldn't comprehend such a thing. And nothing would keep her from drawing battle lines and forcing Bernadette to choose, when—if—Helen found out what had happened with the nanny. Ulysses or Houston. Tyler or Helen.

Bennie would never have to make such a choice and suffer the consequences. Tyler would see to that. He closed his eyes and waded out deeper. Water lapped at his thighs. He would just have to find somebody, anybody, and soon. Helen flew in at Stoney's airstrip tomorrow afternoon for her first visit/ checkup. Surely he could find somebody by then? He had connections. A few calls and he could have somebody here by late morning. She wouldn't be a Dalton woman, but he would just have to make do. Any nanny was better than no nanny at all.

OKAY, so he wasn't the devil, Lucky concluded after drinking in every incredible inch of his backside, from broad shoulders to narrow waist, to the most gorgeous rear end she'd ever seen. She'd only had a glimpse when he'd tossed off his clothes and headed for the water. But now that he stood in the shallow part of the river, she had a much better view. He was definitely just a man. A very *naked* man. *Oh, boy.*

He had buns that put Mel Gibson's to shame.

She blinked, but he didn't disappear. *They* didn't disappear. Tight, tanned, muscular and curved just so...

And lethal to her sanity, she decided as she glanced down and saw that she'd stepped from the shelter of trees. She inched backward and took cover behind a thick tree trunk. Peering around the tree's edge, she directed her attention back to him.

To *them*.

She couldn't help wondering what kind of workout would yield such spectacular results. Undoubtedly a rigorous one, with a lot of flexing, pumping, grinding... A Flex Your Fanny video? A Terrific Tush workout seat? Probably some pumping and grinding of an entirely different nature.

Water rippled and she shrank back behind the tree just as the man stared over his shoulder. All she needed was to be caught trespassing. From what she'd seen of Ulysses, the county seat and home to the world's largest pecan, she'd be strung up to the nearest tree—

Her thoughts ground to a halt as her eyes riveted to his face. It wasn't so much that he was handsome. He was, in a Marlboro man sort of way. Rugged, tough... But more than anything, he was...male. There was nothing feminine about his strong jaw, firm lips, chiseled nose. And his eyes... She couldn't see the color, but somehow she could feel their heat. The heat when a man looks at a woman *that* way. The way Rhett looked at Scarlett. The way Romeo looked at Juliet. The way Buster looked at anything with breasts bigger than his. But Tight Tush wasn't looking at a woman, he was looking at *her,* and she felt that gaze head-on for the first time in her life.

Panic bolted through her and she even stopped chewing her

gum for an endless moment. Surely he'd seen her. He looked
as if he'd seen her. She felt as if he'd seen her.

Infinite seconds ticked by until his gaze passed the spot
where she hid. Then he turned back around. Lucky resumed
her chewing. Of course he hadn't been looking *at* her. He
didn't even know she was there. Story of her life.

Reason kicked in and she inched backward. She had to get
out of there before he really did catch a glimpse of her, not
to mention that she had a wallet to return. Time was money.
But then he scooped up several handfuls of water, doused them
onto his body and she lost what little common sense she had.

The muscles in his arms rippled, catching gleaming rays of
sunlight. Water streamed over his shoulders, down the curve
of his back and those spectacular buns. She'd wind up dangling from the nearest tree for sure, but at least she'd die a
happy woman. Lucky wiped at another trickle of sweat. Hot.
Miserable. Thank God she'd brought an extra pack of chewing
gum, otherwise her throat would be sandpaper—

Pop!

The bubble burst. Gum flattened against her face. And Tight
Tush jerked around. Lucky ducked back behind the tree trunk,
snatched the gum from her mouth and threw it away disgustedly. How could she have forgotten about it? Because she'd
been chewing gum for ages, a habit that even hypnosis hadn't
been able to cure. She was addicted. And stupid, she thought
as she clamped her eyes shut and held her breath.

Water rippled, but otherwise, she heard no sound. Nothing,
just her own breathing and the frantic beat of her heart. She
kept her eyes closed, her back glued to the tree, out of his
sight. Maybe she'd finally lucked out. Maybe he hadn't seen
her. Lord knew she was due…

Her skin prickled with the strange awareness that someone
was watching her and she changed her mind. She'd been
caught in the act. A Peeping Tom. She could read the head-
lines now: Love-Starved Cabbie Resorts To Spying On Unsuspecting Men—

"Enjoying the view?" The slow drawl, rich and deep and slightly amused, slid into her ears.

Lucky's heart stalled, only to rev full speed ahead when she lifted one lid a fraction and saw a pair of large, tanned feet, the toes mere inches from the tips of her sneakers.

Her one eye opened farther and her gaze traveled up a pair of muscular legs encased in faded and slightly damp jeans. The material molded every muscle, showing off his lean calves, powerful thighs. Her gaze hit his zippered fly that was only half zipped, and stopped for a long moment. A wave of heat rushed to her cheeks and she forced her other eye open to get the full view. Not that she actually saw *it*, not that she wanted to, of course. Where the metal teeth parted, she saw only tanned skin and a funnel of dark, silky hair that swirled up over an incredibly tight abdomen. But the sight was enough to make her swallow. Hard.

"I guess you are." Tyler folded his arms across his chest and swept his gaze over the woman. At least he thought it was a woman. It was hard to tell, dressed as she was in faded baggy jeans— He did a double take. Make that unfastened jeans.

He stored that information for safekeeping and pushed his attention higher to the T-shirt plastered to her chest. The white material clung to her, outlining small but perfectly shaped breasts. Her nipples swelled, stretching the material to taut little points and he did some heavy-duty swallowing of his own. Okay, it wasn't that hard to tell. Definitely a woman.

"W-what?"

Her question forced his gaze to the final frontier. Her hair lay hidden beneath her cap, with the exception of a few dark tendrils collapsed against the slender curve of her neck. Her cheeks were flushed from the heat, her pink lips parted, her face damp with perspiration.

"I'm sorry," she went on. Wide eyes the color of warm cocoa collided with his. "I didn't hear you."

He smiled. "I asked if you were enjoying the view." But

Tyler was doing a little enjoying of his own. Not so much from the sight of her, even though that was agreeable enough. No, it was the way she looked at him. Like a child eyeing the last cookie, the want plain and undisguised in her big brown eyes, and she didn't even know the size of his bank account. Of course, his money wasn't all women were interested in. He'd met some who just wanted a roll in the hay. But this one was different. Mixed in with that hungry light was an innocence he hadn't seen in a long time. And with all that hungry innocence directed at him, his jeans grew awful snug in certain strategic places.

"So are you?" he asked, shifting his stance to give a specific body part a little more room.

"Yeah—I mean no. I mean…" She shook her head. "Yes, the view was—is nice, but that's not why I'm standing here."

"Really? Then why are you standing here?"

"I had a flat tire on the dirt road back there." She turned and pointed, but couldn't quite make up her mind in which direction. "Some dirt road. Anyway, I'm not sure where it's at now. That's why I'm here. I'm lost."

"Lost? So that's why you were spying on me?"

"Exactly—no, not exactly. Look, I heard water and thought I might find someone who could steer me in the right direction."

"So why didn't you ask me for directions instead of hiding behind this tree?"

"I wasn't hiding." He raised his eyebrows and watched her face flush an even brighter crimson. "Okay, so I was hiding."

"Not a very effective way to get directions. I would have come right out and asked."

"Oh, really? You'd ask a naked stranger for directions?"

"I would if the naked stranger were me."

"But that doesn't make any sense. You can't be your own naked stranger."

"Good point. Let's see, who could be my naked stranger?" He stepped closer, one arm shooting out to lean against the tree. He gazed at the unfastened button on her jeans. "Wait a second. *You* could be my naked stranger."

"What are you talking—" She glanced down. "Uh-oh."

"Planning on joining me in my nakedness?"

"Of course not." She closed her eyes and shook her head. "Great. This is just great."

"Not yet, but it could be."

Her eyes snapped open. "What?"

"This—you and me—two naked strangers."

"I think one naked stranger is enough." She grabbed at her waistband with frantic fingers.

"Here. Let me."

"No, that's all right. This always happens to me—" His fingers brushed hers. Flesh met flesh and her hands stilled. Their gazes locked as they waited to see what he would do next.

Another breathless moment and Tyler slid the button into place. The action seemed to relax her. Relief eased her expression. "Do you always walk around with your pants undone?"

"My pants, my shoelaces, a few buttons on my shirt." She gave him a look that said she'd given the subject a great deal of thought. "I try, but it seems I'm always missing something."

"That must be quite a sight. A shame you're not from around here."

"No, it's fortunate." She blew out a long breath. "Geez, but it's hot here. Speaking of which, where is here?"

"Here is private property."

"Oh." As if she'd been caught with her hand in the cookie jar, instead of simply ogling the cookie, she added, "I'm sorry. If you'll point me in the right direction, I'll be going."

"I thought you didn't ask naked strangers for directions?"

"You're not naked. Not anymore."

He glanced down at his bare chest. "Almost."

"Well, almost isn't naked." She ducked under his arm and moved around him. "Is it?"

"No, but it's close enough." He turned toward her, closing the few inches of distance she'd opened between them.

"I could scream."

"You could, but what for? Because I'm a stranger, or because I'm almost naked?"

"Maybe both."

"But I'm not the stranger here. You are. Besides," he said, holding up his hands. "I never molest trespassers. Shoot them maybe. But never molest them." His words drew a smile from her. "So tell me, how did you get this far off the road?"

"I was looking for a tree. One tree." She laughed. "Now I'm surrounded by them."

"Well, to get unsurrounded, you head that way." He pointed to his left. "Straight through those trees about five minutes, then you'll be in open pasture. You'll see the road from there."

"Thanks."

"My pleasure."

"No," she said over her shoulder as she started off through the trees. "It was definitely my pleasure. You've got a great set of buns."

"I wish I could say the same." But her jeans were too baggy and he couldn't quite make out any curves. And that was the real shame, he thought as he watched her disappear between two towering oaks, because it had been quite a while since Tyler Grant had wanted to look. Really wanted to look. *Damn*.

If he'd had even half the wild child left in him, he'd have coaxed her out of those pants and seen for himself. But sixteen years away had tamed the hellion he'd once been. At thirty-two, he was exactly what his mother had always wanted him to be: a gentleman. Funny thing was, Tyler Grant had never regretted it until now.

2

WHEN LUCKY finally broke free from the trees, she saw her cab on the horizon. Breathless moments later, she vaulted over the fence and stared behind her. The pasture was empty, the grass swaying with the faint breeze. Not a sign of Tight Tush.

Unfortunately, her hormones whispered.

Thankfully, her brain corrected. As if he would have followed her in the first place. He'd been flirting. Just innocent flirting. She'd seen it time and time again.

But no one had ever directed any flirting at her and she was still a little shaken up over it. More so because she'd liked it. Yeah, she'd liked it a lot, she thought, climbing into the cab.

She definitely had to step up her manhunting efforts. Maybe if she smiled a little, invested in one of those push-up bras, she might persuade Buster— Wait a minute. Buster?

Yeah, Buster, her desperate hormones insisted. He was nice enough, maybe a little crass. He didn't do drugs, though she often wondered, considering how clueless he was when it came to the opposite sex. He was sweet at times. Funny. Obnoxious.

Available, her hormones chimed in. And gainfully employed, and that's all Lucky really needed.

That, and to find Tyler Grant, she thought as she shot a glance at the wallet sitting next to her on the seat.

She'd barely started the engine when she heard sirens. She glanced in her rearview mirror to see a cloud of dust on the horizon and a set of whirling red and blue lights. The sheriff's car pulled up behind her in a matter of seconds.

Lucky killed the engine when two uniform-clad officers climbed out of the car. One was a large man, intimidating in his starched beige uniform and wide-brimmed hat. Straight out of an old *Smokey and the Bandit* movie. She adjusted her rearview mirror to get a glimpse of his sidekick. He looked friendlier, his expression mildly curious as he licked an ice-cream cone.

"Can I see some ID, miss?" It was Smokey, leaning down, peering into the driver's window to capture her in the glare of his aviator sunglasses.

"You guys should have been here an hour ago," Lucky said, handing him her identification and proof of insurance. "I wouldn't have had to lug the spare out of the trunk myself."

"This is an Illinois license, miss, and it's expired."

"Oops. I forgot." One hand dived into the leather pouch hooked onto her radio knob. She rummaged through a mess of receipts, several sticks of chewing gum, a few tissues, until she finally found a crumpled slip of paper. "Here's the current license. I'm new here. Transplanted from Chicago." She gave him a wide smile.

His expression didn't even crack.

So much for southern hospitality.

Smokey scoured the papers, and Lucky had the sudden urge to check her speedometer. But she hadn't been speeding. The car hadn't even been moving. So why did she feel so guilty?

A glimpse of naked flesh and rippling muscles flashed in front of her and her face grew hot. Her gaze cut to Smokey. Did he know? Had Tight Tush actually reported her for trespassing? He'd been so nice, so helpful, so...well, naked. She wiped a trickle of sweat from her temple. She hadn't seen a cellular phone. Actually, she hadn't seen much of anything besides—

"Long way from Houston," Smokey said.

"Just four hours. Is there something wrong, Officer?"

Silence stretched between them while Smokey handed her back her ID. "No," he started, his gaze sweeping the interior of the car. "We've had some trouble nearby so we're checking out all suspicious-looking vehicles—" The words stalled when those mirrored glasses came to rest on the wallet next to her.

"I think you'd better step out of the car. Now. We just caught you red-handed, missy."

Lucky closed her eyes at Smokey's words. How much time could she get for trespassing? Spying? Surely a fine was the most they could give her. "Look, this is all really just a big misunderstanding. I know I shouldn't have climbed the fence, but I had no choice. The diet soda just ran right through me."

"What the hell are you talking about?" Smokey demanded.

"Trespassing. That is why you're here, isn't it?"

"Hell, no, miss. We're here about a burglary. The perpetrator was last spotted headed down this road, out of town."

"Burglary?" Was Tight Tush really a burglar? An escapee from the local prison farm? "He didn't look like a dangerous criminal." Okay, maybe dangerous, she amended silently. Very dangerous, to her sanity, that is.

"You're under arrest."

"Me? But I just had to go to the rest room. And there he was. I couldn't help but look. Had I known he was a hardened criminal..." Her mouth went dry at the fitting vision the words conjured. "Er, that is, a criminal, I would have gone first thing to the cops. I swear—"

"Tell it to the judge." Smokey reached for handcuffs.

"But I didn't do anything wrong. You can't arrest me for unwilling spying. I did trespass, but it was an emergency and—"

"You're not under arrest for trespassing or spying, missy. You're under arrest for burglary." He motioned to the wallet his sidekick had picked up from the front seat.

"But I didn't steal that. I found it."

"Check for a weapon, Billy," Smokey told the sidekick.

"I don't have a gun!" she insisted. When he went to snap the handcuffs on her wrists, she tried to jerk free. "This is crazy! I was only taking a little leak, then a little peek, and I certainly didn't rob anyone! This is unlawful arrest!''

He snapped first one cuff on, then the other, before whirling her to face the cab. "Evidence doesn't lie. A wallet and several other items were reported stolen by Mr. Tyler Grant and we just found you in possession of that wallet." He started to pat her down and Lucky's face flamed hotter. He reached her sides and she erupted into a fit of giggles.

"Ahhhhhh! Please! Stop it," she begged, choking when tears started in her eyes. Another pat, another suppressed giggle and Smokey held up a pack of bubble gum. "I didn't know gum was considered dangerous in this state," she snorted, her eyes still watering, nerves still tingling.

"Quiet, missy. You find anything else besides the wallet?" he asked Billy. "Any of the other stuff?"

"A couple of packs of chewing gum, an air freshener, a flashlight. Back seat's clean."

"Maybe she hid the rest, or ditched some of it when she saw us coming. Dammit, I told Tyler not to bring no city woman out here. Steal you blind if you ain't careful."

"But I didn't steal that wallet. I was returning it!"

Smokey didn't acknowledge her frantic words. He slammed and locked the cab's doors, then shoved her keys into his pocket.

"I'm innocent! I was bringing the wallet back. *Back!*"

"Just calm down, ma'am," Billy said as he stepped forward, a puzzled look on his face. "Didn't Tyler say she hightailed it out of here in Mitchell Pike's old Chevy?" His gaze swept the cab. "This don't look like Pike's old rattletrap to me."

"Criminals ditch stolen cars all the time," Smokey said.

"You've been watching too many 'Adam-12' reruns," Billy told Smokey. "What criminal in their right mind would trade Pike's Chevy for a cab? Sort of conspicuous if you ask me."

"Nobody asked you," Smokey grumbled. He guided her

into the back of the waiting patrol car. "If Tyler wanted some-one to teach his daughter how to be a lady," Smokey went on, "he should've hired Merline over at the Piggly Wiggly. The woman's about as ladylike as you can get. Carries a linen handkerchief to church, and cooks the meanest fried chicken…"

Merline? The Piggly Wiggly? *Burglary?*

It wasn't hell she'd landed in. It was the Twilight Zone. A weird, twisted episode Texas style. She half expected to hear Rod Serling's deep voice, with the "Yellow Rose of Texas" playing in the background.

Not that even one moment of this nightmare actually sur-prised her, not with her never-ending string of rotten luck. But she was in Texas, of all places, and Texans were supposed to be nicer, weren't they?

More like kookier, from the looks of things. Way kooky.

"This is crazy," she said as the car sped down the road. "You can't arrest me when I haven't done anything."

"Maybe she's telling the truth," Billy said as he turned to Smokey. "Don't forget Pike's truck."

"We found her with the evidence, Billy. Tyler reported his wallet stolen by a woman, a *strange* woman, not from around here. Can't get any stranger than her."

"Have you looked in the mirror lately, fella?" Lucky's words earned her a quick glare.

"Could be like she said." Billy glanced at her. "Got kind of an honest face, don't you think? Honest eyes? And what burglar in her right mind would swipe a cab for a getaway car?" Billy shook his head. "Come on, Hank. The chief'll be some kind of mad if he has to postpone his fishing trip for nothing."

"Doggone it." Smokey shook his head. "Oh, all right. If it'll shut you up, I'll take her out to Tyler's first." The car nosed for the shoulder, then made a complete turn.

"Finally some justice," Lucky said. Tyler Grant could tell these bozos she wasn't the robber, she could return his wallet, ask for her eighty-dollar fare and get the hell out of Dodge. Or Ulysses. Or wherever she was.

They drove a good twenty minutes before she spotted the house, a sprawling one-story structure set at least a half mile back from the road. A lush green lawn surrounded the place. Several trees stood tall and proud, their large, lazy branches shielding the surrounding yard from the blinding sunlight.

It wasn't one of those fake mansion-style homes. No, this place looked lived in. It made you think of homemade apple pie and picnics. Just the sort of place that should have a bunch of kids racing back and forth across the grass. A few swings hanging from the trees. Bicycles on the huge porch out front. A cozy wicker love seat just the right size for Lucky and a certain naked stranger...

The car made a sharp turn, effectively killing the vision. They jerked to a stop outside the house. Smokey climbed from behind the wheel and stomped to the front door.

"Chicago," Billy started. "Why, I bet they got all kinds of ice-cream flavors, being a big city and all..."

Smokey disappeared inside the house and Lucky was left listening to Billy discuss the merits of wild raspberry delight versus chocolate fudge ecstasy.

"Here they come," Lucky said when Smokey appeared in the doorway. Lucky tried to stare past him to the man that followed, but she couldn't make out more than a tanned arm here and there, a jeans-clad thigh, scuffed boots.

"Seems you're off the hook, missy," Smokey grumbled as he yanked open the door, pulled Lucky from the seat and unlocked the cuffs. "Tyler here says you ain't the thief."

"At least someone around here has some sense—" The words died when she turned to find herself staring up at the delicious naked stranger with the unforgettable buns. "*You!* You didn't tell me *you* were Tyler Grant."

"I didn't know you were looking for him."

"Well, yes. I found his—your—wallet this morning."

"This reunion's sweet and all," Smokey cut in, "but Billy

and I got a burglar to catch." He tipped his hat at Tyler and said, "Keep you posted."

"Wait a second." She whirled as the car doors slammed shut. "You guys have my keys—" The rest of her sentence drowned in the rev of an engine. The police car bolted down the driveway, gravel spewing from the rear tires.

"*I* have your keys," came the deep voice behind her. "And relax. I'll give you a ride back as soon as you tell me how you got my wallet."

"Like I told Smokey, I found it in the back of my cab." She turned to find Tight Tush staring at her with his heated eyes. Mesmerizing blue eyes as deep as the Caribbean. The kind of blue you could wade waist-deep through and still see your toes. She forced her gaze from his to look at the rest of him. He was far from *au naturel* now, yet he looked every bit as Marlboro-man masculine with his denim shirt, faded jeans and worn cowboy boots. A far cry from Buster and his bowling buddies.

"So you found my wallet?"

"In the back of my cab after I dropped off your wife."

"My *wife?*" Incredulity etched his features for a shocked moment. "Well, how do you like that?" he finally said. Then he burst out laughing. But it wasn't a happy sound. Anger flashed in his eyes, turning them a deep, fathomless turquoise. "Beautiful. Just friggin' beautiful."

"She was."

"Who?"

"Your wife."

"Honey, she wasn't my wife."

"But she was carrying your wallet and..." Her sentence trailed off as Smokey's voice echoed in her mind...*burglary*. "You mean she was—I've been carrying around hot property?"

"Scorching, but the wallet wasn't the only thing she ripped off. She took the entire contents of my safe. Nearly fifty thousand dollars' worth of money and jewelry. Hightailed it out of here before daybreak.''

"In Mitchell Pike's truck," Lucky added. "And she headed straight for Houston where she probably ditched the truck. Then I taxied her to the airport for a clean getaway. To top it off, she stiffed me for an eighty-dollar cab fare. I'm an idiot," she muttered, closing her eyes. "I can't believe I fell for the story like a big sap. A heart attack, of all things."

"She had a heart attack?"

"No, her father did, or she said he did. She was racing to catch a plane so she could rush to his side and nurse him back to health like some Florence Nightingale. Why, the lying, conniving, sleazy little—"

"Daddy! Phone!"

Lucky's gaze darted to the open doorway behind him.

Daddy. This mega babe was a dad?

"Daaadeee!" The shrill voice stretched each syllable.

"I'll be right there." A frown creased his features. "I would really like to ask you a few more questions, Miss…I'm afraid I don't know your name."

"Lucky. Lucky Myers."

"Lucky?"

"It's a nickname. Lucretia…Lucky."

Another shrill "Daddy!" from inside and he said, "Please. Come in a few minutes while I take this call, then we'll talk."

He led her inside the house, into a large room. "You can wait here in the library."

Old movie posters were plastered on the dark-paneled walls. There was *Giant, East of Eden, Rebel Without a Cause, The Maltese Falcon, Casablanca, Key Largo* and at least a dozen others. They covered every spare inch not lined with bookshelves. An antique movie projector sat on top of the bookshelf nearest her.

"Wow," she breathed. "Does that work?"

"Supposedly."

"You don't know?"

"I've only been back a few months, and watching old movies hasn't been on the top of my list."

"Where were you before?"

"Houston."

"Home?"

"No" he said a little too sharply and she glanced up to see a strange light in his ocean eyes. "This is home."

She smiled. "It feels like a home. Warm, cozy, though it's bigger than the entire first floor of my apartment building."

"And where is that?"

"Houston, too. But it's not much of a home. Not yet, anyway. But then six months isn't really enough time to get settled. I'm originally from Chicago, born and bred." She blinked at the sudden burning in her eyes and sought a distraction. Her gaze went to a glass cabinet sitting in one corner. Inside sat a cowboy hat and a pair of boots.

"A shrine to the great James Dean," he said as if reading her thoughts. "Rumor has it he wore those in the movie *Giant*."

"You're kidding?"

He shook his head. "My dad swears it." When her gaze went to the movie projector and the rows of old movie reels, he added, "Those are the real thing, too."

"This is great." She trailed her hand over the projector.

"You like old movies?"

"Old, new. I like them all."

"A woman after my dad's heart."

A woman after your heart, she thought, then quickly discarded the notion. A lifetime and she hadn't managed to win anyone's heart. What could she possibly accomplish in the thirty or so minutes before she'd be on her way back to Houston? She was the invisible, flat-chested woman and he was *Playgirl*'s stud of the month. They were on opposite sides of the universe. There was no connection. Nothing.

He smiled, her heart shifted and she averted her gaze lest she salivate right then and there.

"So what about you?" she asked. "You like old movies?"

He shook his head. "I'm not much of a movie buff. In fact, I've been after Dad to do away with some of this stuff, but he's so stubborn."

"But it's great—"

"Daddy! Grandmother's on the phone!"

"Five minutes," he promised Lucky as he headed out of the room. The way her hormones were chanting, she knew they'd be the five longest minutes of her life.

3

"IT'S ABOUT TIME, Daddy." Bernadette Willemina Grant stood in Tyler's study, one hand planted on her hip, the telephone receiver clutched in her other. His twelve-year-old daughter wore a nearly threadbare T-shirt, faded jeans and large black rubber boots that crept halfway up her thighs. Helen would have his hide for sure.

He sat down at his desk and tried not to smile. "What happened to the dress Mabel put out for you this morning?"

"Daddy," she groaned, giving him a what-horse-just-walloped-you-in-the-head? look. "Jed's waiting for me. I'm helping him clean out Liz's stall."

"So you're all done with your schoolwork and piano lessons?"

"Of course not, Daddy."

"Well, shouldn't you be finishing it instead of cleaning out stalls? And honey, you really ought to put on a dress."

She rolled her eyes. "How am I supposed to concentrate, with Liz wallowing around in a stinky stall? And a dress—" she made a face "—I can't help Jed if I'm wearing a dress. Come on, Daddy. Mabel says it's okay if you say it's okay. I told her you would because you've always been a huge supporter of animal rights—"

"Go, but finish your lessons right after dinner, is that clear? And put on something nice when you're done in the barn."

"Thanks, Daddy." She gave him a quick kiss and bolted from the room. Her three-sizes-too-large boots slapped against the hardwood floor and Tyler couldn't help smiling.

"I was just getting ready to hang up," the woman's voice snapped the minute he said hello.

"Sorry you had to wait, but I was in a meeting—"

"That illustrates my point exactly, Tyler. Bernadette needs more attention. Do you know what she wants for a pet? Forget a nice French poodle or a cockapoo. She wants a lizard. Now, I don't have anything against reptiles. I have nearly ten alligator handbags. But my granddaughter wanting to nurture a live reptile causes me a bit of concern. When Nan was twelve, she was looking forward to her coming out. She'd roll over in her grave if she knew what you were allowing her daughter—"

"*Our* daughter, Helen. Nan and I made Bernadette together, and she isn't a Bell-Whitman. She's a Grant."

"My Nan's blood still runs through Bernadette's veins. Now, Tyler, you really should consider sending her back to Houston. Smithston's already agreed to let her start midsemester. They've got one of the best academic programs around and they offer dance lessons, etiquette, fashion coordination—everything Bernadette needs at her age."

"What makes you so sure she isn't already learning everything she needs to right here?"

Helen laughed. "Come now, Tyler. One top-notch governess in no way compares to an entire staff of highly qualified personnel, and Ulysses isn't exactly the social seat."

"There are plenty of social activities here. The Hickory Festival is in two weeks. Competitors come from all over Texas for the pecan pie competition. Then there's the beauty pageant."

Helen ignored him and plunged ahead, sugary sympathy disguising the ever-present steel in her voice. "You know Merle and I understand you're not in Ulysses by choice. We know you had no way of foreseeing your father's illness. But there's no reason to force Bernadette to stay there and share in the misery. I'm sure once you take a look at Smithston's fall schedule, you'll see what Bernadette's missing and change your mind. I'll bring a copy this afternoon.''

"*This* afternoon? You mean tomorrow afternoon.''

"Change of plans, dear. Merle's business meeting in San Antonio has been moved to tomorrow morning at nine.'' Before the news could sink in, she rushed on, "Merle and I are flying in. We'll be there in a little over two hours. In fact, he's waving me off the phone right now. Bye, dear. I can't wait to meet that new Dalton governess you hired.''

Two hours. He had all of two hours to find a governess. Otherwise, he'd have a hell of a fight on his hands. Not that Helen could do more than cause a stink, but what a stink, and Bennie would be caught right in the middle.

He couldn't allow that. No, he wanted Bennie happy. That meant keeping Helen happy and finding a governess. Fast.

He glanced down at his stolen wallet, each bill accounted for, tucked safely away along with his credit cards. His Visa and American Express Gold Card were missing, but he knew Lucky hadn't swiped them. The nanny had obviously pocketed those for frequent use, which was fine by him. He'd already reported the cards missing, and should she try to use them, she would find herself behind bars.

Tyler closed the wallet and trailed his thumb along the smooth leather edge as Lucky's image pushed into his thoughts.

She had the most incredible eyes, so warm and brown, framed by long, thick dark lashes. Though it wasn't her eyes he really remembered. It was the way she'd looked at him with those eyes. He could still feel her gaze on his bare back, sliding down, making his skin tingle…

Too bad he couldn't hire her. But it would never work. Those wide-eyed looks, all that innocence she oozed, were all part of a well-practiced act. Otherwise he wouldn't find himself so attracted to her, would he? And the last thing he needed was a seductress under his roof.

Then again, Ulysses was thirty minutes away. It would take

him an hour to drive to town and back, which left only an
hour to find some unknown somebody. The odds weren't in
his favor. Ulysses had all of six hundred and eighty-two citizens, all fine upstanding people as nice as could be, but he
was fairly certain none of them would be more qualified than
Lucky, seductress or not.

Besides, she was intelligent. He'd seen that in her eyes amid
all the hunger and innocence, and it was only for one evening.
Come morning, Helen and Merle would be on their way to
their business meeting.

Yes, he needed Lucky. In more ways than one, he thought.

That's why it would never work. This was business, purely
business, and Tyler shouldn't be having these kinds of urges
over a business acquaintance—a tomboyish, bigmouthed acquaintance. Besides, Helen wanted a fancy governess from a
fancy agency, and she could smell an ordinary, working-class
Joe quicker than a bloodhound could scent out a rabbit—

His daughter's high-pitched squeal cut into his thoughts,
brought him up out of the chair and over to the window. He
stared across the yard to the huge red and white barn where
Bennie stood out front wielding a water hose.

"I can nail you with one shot, mister!" She smiled and
turned the spray on Jed, a wiry old man who'd been at the
ranch as long as Tyler could remember. Jed returned fire and
Bennie squealed, water soaking her from head to booted foot
until she looked like a wet puppy, all scrawny and vulnerable,
and happy. Yes, she looked happy, and Tyler felt as if someone had landed a boot up against his backside.

A few seconds later, he headed out back to tell Bennie about
Helen's change of plans. Then he'd make Miss Lucky Myers
the offer of a lifetime.

For Bennie, he reminded himself again.

AFTER DEVOURING the titles on all the old movie reels, Lucky
moved on to the numerous bookshelves.

Breeding Cattle. How to Make a Winner. So Mr. Big Bucks

was in the cattle-prostitution business. Obviously it paid better than most escort services if this spread was any indication—

"Bennie!" The shout brought Lucky over to a huge bay window overlooking the back of the house in time to see Tyler Grant face off with a young girl, no more than twelve or thirteen. The Terminator with a water hose.

She aimed her weapon, but Tyler was too quick. The spray barely soaked the back of his shirt before he moved, hefting her over his shoulder in a head-on tackle. She shrieked, squirming in a fit of laughter as he attacked her with tickling fingers.

Lucky smiled, despite the pang of longing that shot through her for a naked stranger who looked really great in a wet shirt—

"Hold it right there, snake woman!"

The book she'd been holding sailed to the floor. Lucky whirled, to find herself staring down the barrel of a very lethal-looking shotgun.

"Now hold on a minute." Her gaze flew to the old man brandishing the gun. Snow-white hair covered his head, the same color as the beard that hid half his face.

Colonel Sanders. She was being attacked by Colonel Sanders.

For a shocking moment, her gaze riveted on the bandages covering both his eyes.

Make that a *blind* Colonel Sanders.

Panic bolted through her and she forced a calming breath. If he couldn't see, he couldn't aim, and that meant she had a chance. "Just calm down, mister. You—you've got the wrong person."

"Shut your lyin' mouth! You might've put one over on my boy, but I knew you was rotten from the get go, missy."

The tip of the barrel wavered, and Lucky inched sideways several feet. Her thigh came up hard against the glass case holding the James Dean boots and hat. Wood creaked and the man swung around. The barrel streaked through the space between them and crashed into the shelf holding the old movie projector.

Wood splintered, the projector hit the floor, metal pieces clanged and rolled, and the man let loose a string of violent curses.

"Dadblame it, sonofa—"

"Dad! Put that gun down!" Tyler strode through the doorway, his hair a tangled, dripping mess. He had a white towel draped around his neck, his shirt and trousers soaked and streaked with mud.

She sniffed, wrinkling her nose. It smelled more like fertilizer or horse doo—

"Good Lord," breathed the short pudgy woman with gray hair and wide gray eyes who rushed in after Tyler.

Tyler's eyes flashed anger and outrage as he reached the old man. His hands went to the wayward shotgun and the gnarled fingers gripping the handle. *"What the hell are you doing?"*

"Trying to give this yellow-bellied thief what she deserves." The old man resisted, playing tug-of-war with his larger, obviously stronger son. "She thought she could put one over on us, boy. But I ain't letting her get away with it."

"Give up the gun right now," Tyler ordered, the words soft, yet steely. "I mean it."

"Aw, go on and take the blasted thing." The old man released the weapon and let Tyler steer him to a chair. "Tried to warn you, boy. You cain't trust no woman who calls a fourteen-point buck *precious*. It just ain't natural."

"Give me the keys to the gun cabinet, Dad."

"Didn't get it from no gun cabinet." The old man crossed his arms, his mouth set in a pout that resembled a stubborn child's. "That there's my own personal protection. Keep it under my bed for just such emergencies."

"You could've caused one hell of an emergency if you'd pulled the trigger." When the old man held his stance, Tyler added, "Give them to me." The man looked ready to refuse, but after a long, tense moment, he dropped the keys into Tyler's outstretched hand. Something dangerously close to regret flashed in Tyler's eyes before he smiled. "Keep him out of trouble, Mabel," he told the pudgy woman.

"Come on, Ulysses. I just made up a batch of stew."

"Now that's the best thing I heard all day." Ulysses grasped the woman's hand and pulled to his feet, a smile creasing his face. "You wouldn't happen to have some fresh-baked biscuits to go with it?"

"And fresh buttermilk to drink."

"Hot damn, Mabel! My eyes might be shot, but my taste buds are in their prime." The old man's excitement fled as he cast a frown over his shoulder. "Don't turn your back on her. And keep her away from my Jimmy Dean hat and boots." Then he shook his head. "Precious. Of all the blasted things…"

"Don't mind him." Mabel ushered the man out the door. "He's cranky because one of the cable channels is running a twenty-four-hour Clark Gable marathon and he's gonna miss it."

"Oh, well, that explains it then," Lucky said, still dazed from the past few minutes.

"Aw, who cares about those old shows," the man grumbled.

"You do, you stubborn old coot," Mabel said. "Now come on."

"Are you all right?" Tyler's hand went to her arm, his thorough gaze combing her from head to toe.

"I—I think so." She shook her head. "Who was that?"

"That was Tyler Ulysses Grant the first, founder of this ranch and one pigheaded old man. He had double eye surgery a few months ago to correct a retina impairment. When the police car rolled up earlier, everybody here thought Hank had nabbed the thief. My father's a little hot-tempered and I guess he thought he'd get a jump on the justice system. He only meant to scare you."

"Mission accomplished," she mumbled, pulling in a deep breath. "But I think my heart is beating again." Not beating. Pounding. A frenzied rhythm that had started the moment Tyler's long lean fingers had touched her to check for injuries.

Fingers that were still touching her.

"I'll be all right," she said, expecting him to let go. He didn't for a long, drawn-out second. Something simmered in his eyes. That unreadable something she'd seen earlier.

"Why are you staring at me like that?"

"Like what?"

"Like you're ready to swallow me whole."

A grin lifted the corners of his mouth. "Now there's a thought. Though, I have to admit, I usually like to take my time, savor each bite..." His voice trailed off as he studied her with those damnable eyes of his. A drop of water slid down his temple, his strong jaw, and Lucky had the inexplicable urge to reach out and catch the drop. Taste it. Taste him...

He wiped his face with the edge of his towel and Lucky cleared her throat.

"I'm sorry about you getting ripped off and everything. If you'll give me the eighty bucks your nanny stiffed me for, I'll be on my way. I've got a lot of work waiting."

He gave her the once–over, from the top of her baseball cap-covered head, to the ends of her sneakers, before leveling a stare at her. "So how about working for me this evening?"

Before her hormones could start harmonizing "Hallelujah," she blurted out, "I don't think there's a big need for taxi drivers out here in Timbuktu."

"Ulysses," he corrected. "And I don't need a driver. I need a nanny for my twelve-year-old daughter."

She couldn't stop the chuckle that bubbled on her lips. "Do I look like a nanny to you?"

"Not now, but with a little work you could pass. Besides, it's just for a few hours. One evening. The woman you picked up in your cab was my governess, or was supposed to be. She was here all of two days before she cleaned out my safe and took off. Now I need a temporary replacement.''

"Aren't you afraid I might warp your daughter or something? I mean, I know I won't, but you don't. You just met me.''

"You returned a wallet full of credit cards and money, without even deducting your cab fare. That says a lot.'' Frustration darkened his eyes to arctic blue. "Look, Lucky. Here's my situation. My in-laws are arriving today. If they find out about what happened with the real nanny, I'll never hear the end of it. All I need is someone to pose as a nanny tonight while they're here. Just a warm body.''

"No.'' Not that her body wasn't warm at the moment. It was. Dangerously warm. "I'm sorry about what happened and I wish I could help you out, but I can't. Why don't you call a service or take out an ad or something?''

"No time. I need someone now. Someone I can trust.'' He raised desperate eyes to her. "I'm willing to pay, Lucky. Just one evening. I'll teach you enough to get you through a few hours of conversation, my mother-in-law will be happy and I'll be off the hook.''

"How much?''

"Five hundred dollars,'' he said.

"Make it a thousand.''

"I thought you didn't want to do this.''

"I didn't say that. If the price is right, I'll do anything—within reason, of course. This seems reasonable. A little kooky, but hey, you're the one with the thousand bucks and I'm neck-deep in debt.''

"What kind of debt?'' He looked suspicious. "It isn't anything illegal—''

"Nursing-home payments. I have a granny—my dad died last year and I don't have any other family left—and she's at this really expensive nursing home in Houston. Anyhow, they've been letting me slide on the payments since my dad passed away, but now I have to bring the account current. So it's a thousand bucks, or no deal.''

"Okay," he said after a long moment. "A thousand bucks. One evening. You eat dinner, pretend to be the nanny, spend the night and say goodbye to my in-laws at breakfast. That's it.''

"What about my cab fare?"

"A thousand dollars, plus the cab fare."

"And I want half my money up front."

"For someone desperate, you sure make a lot of demands." He nodded. "I'll have to go to the bank." He glanced at his watch. "You can ride to town with me, and I'll drop you by Earline's beauty shop. She can get you fixed up while I take care of things at the bank."

"What about your wife? Since I'm playing this little role for your in-laws, don't you think she might want to give me a look-over before you hire me?"

"She certainly would," he replied. "But she passed away a couple of years ago. A car accident."

Yes!

Yes? What kind of morbid person was she? He'd just admitted a tragedy to her. Granted, a tragedy that made him unattached, but still a tragedy.

"I'm sorry. I didn't mean to pry."

"You didn't. Now, first things first, we need to get you out of those clothes."

Whoa, baby. Was this guy a mind reader or what? She took a deep breath, tried to calm her raging hormones and fished a stick of gum from her pocket.

"No gum chewing." He plucked the gum from her hand and motioned to her pocket. "Give it up."

The money. She handed over the gum and tried not to stare longingly. Just think about the money.

"Do you need to get in touch with your boss and tell him where you'll be?" Tyler asked, drawing her attention.

"I don't have a boss. I'm an independent driver for Speedy

Cab. Which means I work when I want to, pay a flat fee from each fare to the cab company and don't work when I don't want to.''

"Won't someone be worried about you if you're gone all night? Your family? Husband?''

"No,'' she retorted, wishing his words didn't bring the familiar ache to the pit of her stomach. "There's just my granny. No other family. No husband.'' *Hint. Hint.*

"Good—I mean, it's good that we won't be inconveniencing anybody with our little charade.'' He smiled, that slow, lazy, naked-stranger smile that made her heart beat faster and her body go from warm to blazing hot.

Of course, his smiles didn't mean anything, she told herself a few minutes later as she followed him down the hall toward the guest room. The faded denim of his jeans pulled and tugged at all the right places as he walked and Lucky tried to fix her gaze at a point just above his shoulder. She had no doubt that he flirted with every woman. Some men were like that. They oozed sex appeal.

Not that anyone had done any oozing in her direction, mind you. Which was all the more reason for her to take the job. Lucky had quite a few things to learn in the man-woman department if she ever wanted to find that special someone, settle down and have herself an honest-to-goodness family. She intended to finish school first, but meanwhile, she could polish her manhunting skills.

Since Tyler Grant seemed pretty good at attracting the opposite sex, maybe she could learn a thing or two from him while she played nanny to his daughter. How to flirt, at least. He was a master at that, and once she returned to the real world, a push-up bra could only do so much.

FIFTEEN MINUTES LATER, after Tyler had showered and changed, he stood in the guest-room doorway and stared at the woman standing near the brass bed. A knock-'em-dead *woman.*

The baseball cap lay discarded atop one frilly Victorian-lace pillow. Jeans, sneakers and T-shirt lay in a heap near the floor-length mirror.

His gaze fixed on the creamy expanse of skin at her ankle, up one sweetly curved calf, then knee, before the image disappeared beneath the hemline of a straight black skirt that hugged every inch of thigh and hip to perfection.

"You can't really mean to make me wear this?" She fingered the extravagant lace cuff of the cream silk blouse she wore, her gaze going to the plunging vee, before sweeping down to the very fitted skirt. "I feel like an overstuffed sausage."

"The other nanny left those behind. She was a little smaller than you."

"Obviously, Sherlock."

His gaze swept her up and down. "I'll go get Mabel. A few safety pins and a seam ripper, and she can fix whatever ails you. Once she's done, you'll look like quite a lady."

She planted stiff fingers on her hips, her narrowed brown eyes pinning him to the door frame. "Meaning I don't look very feminine now?"

"Hold on there, I didn't say you didn't look feminine." He strode over to her. She was definitely tall, coming well past his shoulders. Still, she had to tilt her head to look at him, giving him a full view of her long, slender neck. "You look feminine, all right. No doubt about that."

"And feminine is not ladylike?"

"Not in your case."

"And why is that? Because I don't look like the type of girl you'd take home to Mother?"

"You," he said, trailing a finger down the tempting slope of her neck, "look like the type of gal I'd take home to bed." No sooner had the words left his mouth than he regretted them. *Great, Tyler. Real businesslike. Why don't you just rip her clothes off, do it on the floor and get it over with?*

Shock swept her features, then anger, and Tyler knew he

was in for it. But when she opened her mouth, the only thing in her voice was undisguised curiosity.

"Really? Why?"

He had to laugh at that one. "Are you kidding?"

"No. So what is it about the way I look now as opposed to thirty minutes ago that made you say that?"

Okay, so she was serious. "You look..." His gaze started at her ankles, and moved upward. He couldn't believe they were having this conversation. All of the women in his past had had plenty of self-confidence when it came to looks. Too much. But this woman... She's got it, too, buddy. She's just good at hiding it. At punching your buttons. *It's an act, Sherlock.* A well-played act. Still, when she stared at him so...expectantly, he couldn't seem to keep his mouth shut.

"Curvy," he finally said. "Very curvy. The skirt shows off your legs, your hips." His attention slid higher. "And the blouse... It shows off everything above the waist. Yes, lots of curves. Subtle curves. Just right for a man's hands."

"Curves? Where?"

For an irrational instant, he wanted to eat up the few inches of distance left between them and touch his lips to all the "wheres." But she was his employee for the next twelve hours. His daughter's nanny all of fifteen minutes. And completely off-limits. Great. Now comes the attack of the straitlaced businessman. *Damn.*

"Well?" Impatience edged the word.

"There," he managed to say, his voice gruff as he pointed to the slope of her calves. "All along there." He indicated her legs, long shapely legs. His attention slid higher. "And, of course, there." His jabbed a space in the air to indicate where his attention had finally landed, and a pleased smile lit her face.

"Really? These clothes really make you want to touch me here?" Her hands went to the objects of discussion and he swallowed hard. *Damn. Damn.*

"Geez, and all because of a little blouse," she said. "Forget the push-up bra." Her incredulous voice drew his gaze.

Sexual energy. Potent. Stronger than anything Tyler had ever felt before passed between them. *Damn. Damn. Damn.*

He shook his head as if he could shake away the strange feeling. The strange truth—that he was reacting like a hormone-enraged teenager in the back seat of his daddy's car, and all because of a woman named Lucky, who wore baseball caps, chewed gum and spied on unsuspecting men.

The notion was ridiculous. He was out of his mind, not only to have hired her in the first place, but to actually be lusting after her as though he'd never seen a woman in a tight skirt before.

He'd never seen *this* woman in a tight skirt before, or a silk blouse, for that matter. And she was good, he told himself. It was positively ingenious how she thought to play the innocent virgin. What man could resist such a challenge?

He could. It wasn't as if she had anything that other women didn't, and he didn't have time for games. Lucky was his nanny and Helen was coming.

"We'd better go. We've got a lot to do."

"Yeah," she said, glancing at the mirror one last time before slanting an irresistible grin at him. "You know, I could get used to this."

So could I, his rebellious libido whispered as he left her to go in search of Mabel. *So could I.*

And that was the damned trouble of it all.

4

"WE'RE ALMOST DONE with your hair, sugar. Just hold your head up straight."

Lucky's head bobbed and something bumped her forehead.

"Sorry 'bout that, sugar."

Lucky glanced up as Earline, the owner of Ulysses's only beauty salon, parted bright pink lips and smiled. "They're a work hazard." *They* referred to a pair of double *D*'s squashed beneath a pink knit top. "There," Earline declared, plopping her comb and scissors down to reach for a bottle of styling spritz.

"I don't usually put anything in my hair," Lucky said.

Earline gave her a serious look. "We need height, sugar. To frame your face and bring out those beautiful eyes of yours."

Beautiful eyes. Lucky gave the idea some thought, then smiled. "I've never had height before."

Or breadth, for that matter, she added silently when one of Earline's work hazards bopped her upside the head again.

Ah, breasts... Pointy pyramids to liven up her flat-as-an-Arizona-desert landscape. Breast men would come from all over the world to view in hushed awe. They'd snap pictures to display alongside photos of all the great wonders of the world—the Eiffel Tower, the Taj Mahal... She'd be a universal sex symbol. Yeah, right.

Earline leaned in, her chest bumping the back of Lucky's head again. "Oops, there I go again. Like I said, job hazard."

"Yeah, when it's really cold," came a slightly amused

southern drawl, "Earline can put out an eye with one of those." Doris, Earline's assistant, stood squeezing perm solution on a fifty-something-year-old customer.

Earline glared at the younger woman then turned back to Lucky. "Are you married, sugar?"

"No, but I intend to work on that when I get back to Houston."

"Well, remember one thing when you start hunting for a man. The eyes are everything. My Roger wasn't the best-looking boy back in high school, but he sure knew how to look at a woman. Why, I nearly passed out the first time he looked at me."

"The whole town nearly passed out the first time you looked back," Doris offered. "You were Miss Hickory Honey, for heaven's sake, and he was the class geek."

"Hickory Honey?" Lucky asked.

"The town's yearly beauty pageant. It's the kickoff for the pecan festival that starts in two weeks." Doris pointed to a neon pink flier taped on the wall. "Despite all the ranch land around here, we've got acres and acres of pecan trees. We're the hickory capital of Texas."

Earline sighed. "Being Miss Hickory Honey was the second biggest thrill of my life."

"What was the first?" Lucky asked.

"The first time Roger and I... Well, you know, sugar."

No, she didn't know. That was the trouble.

After Earline had blown and spritzed and brushed until Lucky felt dizzy, the woman reached for what looked like a tackle box.

"Now on to the makeup," she declared. "We'll just widen your eyes a little." She leaned in, wielding a mascara brush the way a Samurai did his sword.

"I think my eyes are wide enough," Lucky said, blinking frantically as the brush came at her.

"Nonsense. Wide eyes are sexy, sugar. Now hold 'em open."

After five unsuccessful attempts, Lucky finally managed not to blink. The mascara went on, then a light dusting of powder and blush. Earline finished with a little lipstick, then stood back to survey her work.

"Ready, sugar?"

For all Lucky's excitement, she couldn't squash the sudden apprehension. She'd never been in a full-service beauty salon before. Most of her haircuts had been at Jake's Barbershop back in Chicago. No spray spritz or blow-dryers. And forget the makeup. Of course, that alone probably accounted for her nonexistent love life.

The chair swung around and Lucky found herself staring at a complete stranger. Soft layers of short brown hair framed the stranger's face. Mascara accented obscenely long eyelashes and gave deep cocoa brown eyes an exotic look.

Exotic. The word echoed through her head and Lucky reached up, her fingers trailing over the soft curls accenting her cheekbones. Her cheekbones. Not some stranger's. This was really her face. Her hair. Her exotic eyes.

"You like it, sugar?"

"Yes," she whispered, her throat closing around the word. "You're a genius, Earline."

"I wouldn't go that far. Oh, hell, maybe I would." The bell on the front door tinkled. "But now comes the real test."

Lucky turned to see Tyler walk through the door. He stopped dead in his tracks, an unreadable expression on his face.

"Well?" she asked. She sat up straighter, her chest pushing up and out a fraction, as if he would notice. But a girl had to try. "What do you think, um, er…Mr. Grant?"

Her words seemed to penetrate his frozen exterior. He blinked and a serious expression passed over his features. He glanced at his watch. "I think we'd better hurry. We've got forty-five minutes and you still have to meet Bennie."

While Lucky stifled her disappointment and climbed from the chair, Tyler paid the bill. He gave Earline a sizable tip and

Doris a smile that would have melted every snowflake during Chicago's worst blizzard.

Not that it bothered Lucky. She knew Tyler Grant was one of *those* men, the experienced kind who flirted with every woman, otherwise he would never have turned all that charm on her.

Experienced. Exactly the sort of man to teach her a thing or two. She focused on that possibility and ignored the strange tightening in her stomach. Experienced was good. Just what she wanted. She only wished he wasn't beefing up his résumé right in front of her.

"HERE'S YOUR MONEY." Tyler handed her an envelope once they'd climbed into Jed's battered Ford pickup that had a giant *R* emblazoned on the side. He keyed the ignition. The engine grumbled and knocked and he cursed.

"I told Jed to replace the battery in this thing."

"If it was the battery, it would be more like a grinding noise." She demonstrated. "See? That's nothing like the knocking. It's probably just being a little temperamental. These '79 Fords sometimes do that." When he raised questioning eyebrows to her, she rushed on, "I'm sort of into cars and trucks—anything on four wheels. Trust me on this. Count to five, give it just a little gas and turn the key nice and slow."

He did as she said. The engine purred to life and Lucky shrugged. "What can I say? It's a gift."

"Thanks." He pulled out onto the main strip through town.

"Thank you." She counted the bills, then shot a glance in the side mirror at her reflection. "So what do you think?"

"You look…different."

"Different?" She stared into the side mirror again. "Different in a bad way, or different in a good way?"

"Different in an…appropriate way."

"Oh," Lucky murmured, stifling another pang of disappointment.

Appropriate. It wasn't a "Gee, Lucky, you're drop-dead

gorgeous," but it would have to do. At least he hadn't said *in*appropriate.

One thousand dollars, she told herself when her stomach did the all-too-familiar churning thing again. She could do this. She would do this. She would dance naked on top of the Empire State Building for a thousand dollars.

Okay, maybe not *naked,* but scantily clad. Bra and panties, max. Maybe she'd even throw modesty aside and use a pair of those skimpy bikini panties—

"Let's review." He braked for a stop sign. "Who are you?"

"Lucky Myers, nanny extraordinaire." When he shot her a frown, she amended, "My name is Lucretia Myers. I've been with the Dalton Agency for five years. My most recent assignment was with a low-profile but filthy-rich oilman from Houston, separated from his wife with temporary custody of two teenage girls. He and the girls spent most of their time at a vacation home in Scotland." She frowned. "A *Texas* oilman in Scotland? Did you make this up?"

"Yes. And?"

"Sounds a little far-fetched, if you ask me, but you're the boss." She took a deep breath and recited the spiel she'd memorized during the thirty-minute trip to town. "I've been in Scotland for the past five years—"

"Which is why you seem slightly out of touch."

"That gets me off the hook on any Texas questions, but what about Scotland? The closest I've been to Scotland is sitting front row through *Braveheart.* It was pretty informational, but I only saw it seven times and—"

"Seven? That's all?"

"I was going for eight, but then my dad died and I moved down here. I've been pulling extra shifts at the cab company to hold my own. That doesn't leave much time for movies."

"You could always buy the video."

"And miss seeing Mel up close and personal?" She shook her head, a smile playing at her lips. "That would definitely kill the fantasy. Maybe if I had one of those big-screen TVs, but it would have to be really big to give the same theater effect.''

"So size is important to you?"

Her heart hit a speed bump that turned out to be a major pothole when she looked over at him. He was just so beautiful sitting there, gripping the steering wheel, staring straight ahead as if he'd asked her about something as mundane as the weather. Size, girl. Definitely a flirty comment if she'd ever heard one.

She chose her words carefully. "If you're talking TV screens."

"And if we're not?"

"Then it depends on what we're talking about." She swallowed. "So what are we talking about?"

He grinned. "What do you think we're talking about?"

"That's not fair. You can't answer my question with a question. I asked first. Are we talking screens or...?"

"Or what?" He shot her a smoldering glance, his lips hinting at a grin.

"Men." There, she'd said it.

He nodded. "Actors."

"Actors?" She tried not to sound depressed.

"What else?"

"Actors," she said firmly. "Yeah, actors." She stared through the windshield and searched for a vision of her favorite actor. Instead of seeing a wily Scotsman, she kept picturing a cowboy. A very naked cowboy, with water streaming down his skin and the sunlight playing off his muscles and his... "Definitely a big-screen man," she murmured. "Really big."

"Who?"

"Uh, Mel." She stiffened in her seat. "Yeah, big-screen all the way. Definitely."

"Yeah," he grumbled, and Lucky had the strangest sensation that she'd just disappointed him somehow.

"So back to your mother-in-law. What should I talk about?"

"You don't talk. I'll do all the talking."

"What if she asks me questions about Scotland?"

"She won't. Helen was there once and spent the entire two weeks sick in her hotel room. Allergies, though she'd die before she ever admitted it. Scotland is the one place she doesn't like, so I doubt she'll drill you on the subject."

"I don't know about this." She shook her head, doubts creeping through her, her mouth watering for a piece of gum.

His hand reached across the seat to close over hers. "You can do it, Lucky. Just relax and remember everything I told you."

"Yeah, relax." She took a deep breath and suppressed the disappointment when he returned his hand to the wheel. "I can do this," she said more for herself than him. "It's not as if I'm totally clueless when it comes to educating a child."

"It's just one night," he reminded her. "You won't be educating anyone."

"I do have some college under my belt," she went on as if he'd never said a word. "Liberal arts with a minor in education."

"You're not going to be a real nanny."

"I've had child psychology and all the basics. That's something." She glanced at him. "Isn't it?"

He nodded and smiled. "Let me guess, underneath that rough exterior lurks the heart of a kindergarten teacher."

"More like an auto-shop teacher. I've always liked cars and kids."

"So why are you driving a cab in Houston instead of teaching mechanics to some rowdy kids back in Chicago?"

She shrugged. "My granny. She was originally from Texas, and when she got sick with Alzheimer's, Dad moved her here from Chicago. He wanted to come himself, but I was going to college and working part-time as a mechanic, and he didn't want to leave me. Then he died, the nursing-home payments fell to me, and so did his cab.'' She blinked away the sudden moisture in her eyes. ''Granny is my number-one priority right now. I'll finish school eventually.''

''What about a student loan?''

''Do you know how much shop teachers make? I make more driving my cab. I couldn't swing a new career, nursing-home payments *and* loan payments. It's better to pay as I go, even if it takes a while.'' She turned on him then. ''Would you stop looking at me like that?''

''Like what?''

''Like you feel sorry for me.''

''I do feel sorry for you.''

She stiffened. ''Don't. I don't need your pity.''

He grinned. ''Oh yes you do. You, sweetheart, are about to meet my mother-in-law. I guarantee, fifteen minutes into it, and you'll be begging for my pity.''

''Gee, you're doing wonders for my confidence.''

His grin disappeared. ''Tell me the story again.''

She banged her head against the window. ''*Ugh.* Not again.''

''Again.''

She took a deep breath and tried to focus her thoughts. ''Okay, I've been in Scotland. The oilman got a divorce, his wife got the kids, which ended my assignment. Then the agency sent me here.''

''Exactly. And remember, whatever you do, don't encourage any questions. Just give the barest answers, and I'll pick up any slack in the conversation. Dinner will fill up some of the time, then you can pretend a headache and escape to your room. After that, we'll have tomorrow morning to get through, which shouldn't be too difficult. Merle, that's my father-in-law, is expected at a nine o'clock meeting in San Antonio, which means they'll be in a hurry. Thirty minutes for break-fast, then I'm off the hook and you're on your way back to Houston.''

Simple. Then why did she have the unconscious urge to

start chewing even though the nearest piece of gum was in the glove compartment of her cab?

Geez, her cab. "Where's my Chevy?"

"It's hidden away in the garage near the barn. I sent Jed and one of my part-time hands to pick it up."

"But no one drives my cab but me," she blurted out before she could think about how silly it sounded.

"I thought men were the only ones territorial about their cars."

"I'm not territorial. Not exactly." She took a deep breath. "Okay, maybe a little, but that cab is all I have." All I have left of my father.

"I'm sorry," he said as if he sensed her sudden melancholy. "I should have asked your permission first, but I'm sure Jed didn't hurt it. If so, we'll take him out back and have him whipped." He flashed her that all-too familiar naked-stranger smile, and she couldn't help but grin.

Great buns and a sense of humor. Lord help her.

"So what does the initial stand for?" she asked as they turned into the driveway and passed the gate where an *R* had been fashioned in black iron.

"Reata."

"You're kidding, right?"

He stiffened and shook his head. A strange expression crossed his face and Lucky got the feeling she was prodding old wounds instead of making small talk. "So your father has a thing for the movie *Giant?*"

He nodded.

"Is it the movie in particular, or the fact that James Dean was in it?"

"Both." Everything about the way he sat there, fingers gripping the steering wheel, gaze riveted straight ahead, told her to shut up. To mind her own business.

"Any particular reason why he picked a name from that movie and not some other James Dean flick?" she heard herself asking.

"It had…special significance."

"Oh." Silence fell around them as he braked to a stop and killed the engine.

"Come on. Jed's picking up Helen and Merle right now. You've got just enough time to meet Bernadette before show-time."

Lucky climbed from the truck, teetering dangerously when her heel sank an inch or so into the dirt. Tyler caught her a moment before she pitched forward.

"Maybe I could wear my own shoes tonight."

"Tennis shoes don't go with the outfit. Don't stand up any more than necessary and just relax."

Taking a deep breath, she concentrated on each step. She could do this. For a thousand dollars, for Granny, she could wear the shoes, the hair, the clothes, and do it all without a piece of gum.

"Where's Dad?" Tyler asked Mabel when they entered the house.

"In his room, but he's as grumpy as an old mule since I told him about Helen. Threatened to go after her with his shotgun whenever he manages to find it."

"You have an awfully violent family," Lucky told him.

Tyler shook his head. "Dad's just temperamental." He reached out and trailed a fingertip along Lucky's cheek. "He wouldn't have hurt you."

Her body tingled, and from only the barest touch of his finger. If she ever felt more… A full hand, for instance, an arm locked around her, his lips on hers… She'd be a goner for sure.

As if he'd just realized what he was doing, his hand dropped away. "Hold tight, I'll be right back," he said and left.

Lucky closed her eyes and fervently prayed he would be.

"DAD?" Tyler called out as he walked into his father's bed-room. He came up short in the doorway as he caught sight of Ulysses sitting in his rocking chair, a bowlful of ice cream on

the tray in front of him, and a bottle of Maalox in his hand.
"*Dad!*"

The old man's head snapped around, his bandaged eyes directed at Tyler for a split second before passing him by. He tipped the bottle.

"Put that down!" Tyler reached him in two strides and snatched the bottle out of his hands.

"But I cain't eat no dadblasted ice cream without syrup."

"That's not syrup."

"Sure it is. Mabel put my syrup here on the left and my stomach medicine on the right. Said to take a spoonful right after dinner so's the fried potatoes don't get to me." He groped for the bottle on his right, his fingers skimming over the handle and the sticky strawberry spout. He touched a fingertip to his lips. "Hell, boy, you know my stomach medicine tastes just like Mabel's homemade syrup?"

"That *is* Mabel's syrup."

Ulysses frowned. "Are you telling me I cain't tell the difference between my stomach medicine and my syrup?"

"Exactly."

"Hell, boy. I'm blind. I ain't deaf. Syrup on the left, stomach medicine on the right. I know what I heard."

"You have to be careful." It's a good thing Tyler was here. A damned good thing, otherwise Mabel would be rushing his father to the nearest emergency room to have his stomach pumped, or whatever they did for a Maalox overdose. "Dad," he said gently, "maybe you heard wrong, or maybe Mabel got her left and right mixed up—"

"Damned straight she did."

"Either way, you have to take it slow and easy and be careful about what you put in your mouth." His father could down a bottle of the rat poison Mabel kept in the bottom kitchen cupboard, or take one too many pain pills, or turn his electric blanket on too high and bake himself to death or...a dozen scenarios raced through Tyler's mind. All bad. He shook away the panic. Nothing so tragic was going to happen.

He was here to look out for his dad now and things were going to be A-okay.

"My dadburned eyes." Ulysses stared moodily at his bowl. "I'll never see a dadblasted thing ever again."

Tyler hunkered down beside him. "The bandages will be off tomorrow, and the doctor said there's a ninety-eight percent chance your vision will be back to normal within a week or two."

"What about the other two percent? Pretty flimsy success rate if you ask me." He snorted. "Damn city doctors. Cain't trust a one of 'em. Just after the insurance money. That fancy-schmancy surgeon's probably lying on some beach in some foreign country, sipping one of those fruity drinks with the little umbrellas, while I'm sitting here blind, and with a ranch falling apart around me."

"I'm taking care of the ranch."

His dad's frown vanished and a smile eased the lines around his eyes. "And doing a hell of a job, son. I don't know what I'd do without you." He patted Tyler's hand, then the smile gave way to another frown. "Now, if that old busybody mother-in-law of yours would keep her nose out of our business, things would settle down just right." He grabbed his spoon to jab at his ice cream. "But no, she has to come running out here to mess things up." He shoved a spoonful of ice cream into his mouth and swallowed. "And damn near dinnertime, too." He waved the spoon at Tyler. "She'll be sitting at my table, crowding my space. Why, I got just the right amount of elbow room as it is."

Tyler swallowed. "I think you're going to have even less."

"How's that?"

"Well, it's like this, Dad." Tyler launched into a quick explanation of the turn of events and Lucky's new role as nanny. He ended with an optimistic "It's just for one night."

"One night too many," his dad grumbled. "Forget the fried potatoes. Pass me the Maalox, son. I think I need a shot now."

WHILE TYLER talked to his dad, Lucky spent fifteen minutes waiting and debating whether to sit or stand. She alternated between both, then the urge hit her. She'd had two more sodas at Earline's and her kidneys were working overtime.

After a quick bathroom trip, she made her way back down the hallway. Passing the library, she spotted the shattered projector, the pieces still scattered across the hardwood floor.

Before she could stop herself, she walked inside. There was just something about mechanical parts that said come and get me, baby. She preferred car engines, but other things—appliances, TVs, even old movie projectors—held the same appeal. The challenge. Lucky could fix anything. Almost anything, she thought, spying the pieces. This might prove more difficult.

Not that she had the time to fix the projector, she amended. She wouldn't be here long enough to really sink her teeth into the project. She was a temporary nanny. A one-night stand.

Ah, well, a girl had to start somewhere.

A quick glance at the clock and she slipped off her shoes, hiked up her skirt and got on her hands and knees. Grabbing a nearby ashtray, she started gathering parts.

Five minutes later, she was ready to call it quits, when she spotted the camera lens. Setting the ashtray aside, she climbed under the desk and reached for it.

"What are you doing?"

Tyler's voice froze her hand a fraction shy of her goal. Her head shot up, slamming into solid wood, and she screeched.

"Are you all right?" He knelt beside her, so close she backed into him when she tried to scoot out. Her bottom touched one hard thigh and heat shot through her, effectively refocusing her thoughts from her throbbing head to her throbbing hormones.

"I'm fine," she managed to say, dragging in a deep breath before she scooted a few more inches out and away from him. "These parts were just lying here and it seemed a shame... Geez, you scared the daylights out of me." She turned an accusing gaze on him. "Is this a trait that runs in your family?"

"What?"

"Sneaking up on innocent, unsuspecting guests."

"Innocent, huh?" One eyebrow lifted and his gaze darkened to a deep blue as he stared at her stocking-clad legs. The skirt had slid a few inches higher and the hem straddled her upper thighs. "You don't look so innocent to me."

"Really?" She smiled, catching and holding his gaze, drinking in the feeling those eyes gave her when they stared at her the way he was staring at her now. She felt power. She felt desirable. She felt like a wom—

"Tyler? Bernadette?" The slam of the front door punctuated the woman's voice. "We're here!"

"Damn!" Tyler growled. "They're early." He climbed to his feet and pulled Lucky up beside him.

"Come on," he said, yanking her along after him.

"But my skirt..." She pulled away from him and jerked at the hem. Tyler turned, and in one smooth motion swept the fabric down her thighs, leaving a sizzling path where his fingers had grazed her.

"Tyler!" The voice moved closer and panic swamped Lucky. "Where in the world...?"

One thousand dollars, she recited to herself. If she just concentrated on the words, she could do this. *One...*

"Your shoes," Tyler said.

She whirled, scrambling for one pump while he reached for the other.

thousand...

"Tyler Grant!" came the voice, slightly irritated and dangerously closer.

"Here." He shoved one shoe on her foot, helped her on with the other, then hauled her out into the hallway just as a woman rounded the corner.

dollars. But it wasn't enough, she realized as she stared at the older woman, into eyes as cold and assessing as the principal's who'd nearly expelled her for chewing gum in the third grade. Then Tyler stepped up behind her.

"You look different," he whispered, his voice deep and steady and soothing, "in a good way."

And Lucky managed a wobbly step forward.

5

"HI, I'M LUCK—retia Myers." Lucky thrust out her hand. "It's a pleasure to meet you."

"I'm Helen Bell-Whitman. I take it you're the governess Tyler has been telling me about?"

"Yes, ma'am."

Cold black eyes swept Lucky from head to toe before shifting their attention to Tyler. "The first time I arrive for a visit, and no one has the decency to meet me at the door."

"You're ten minutes early," he replied smoothly, obviously not the least bit intimidated by her Big Bad Mother-in-law stare.

"The flight in was smooth," Helen went on. "We made excellent time."

"Where's Merle?" Tyler asked.

"Still out in the car. An important business call came just as we arrived. I'm sure he'll be along shortly. So this is Reata." Her disapproving gaze swept the paneled interior of the hallway. "This can't be much larger than our guest house."

"This house is over five thousand square feet with six bedrooms," Tyler told her.

"Atrociously small," she sniffed with disdain.

"Can we at least wait until after dinner before we start arguing?"

"I never argue, dear. I was simply pointing out that Bernadette would be much better off back home—"

"This is her home, Helen. Speaking of Bernadette, Miss Myers was just going to fetch her."

"I was?" Lucky asked, then Tyler gave her a discreet nudge. "Oh, yes, yes. I was."

Which way? Lucky's brain screamed as she cast desperate glances in either direction.

As if Tyler had tuned in to her frequency, he touched her arm, just the slightest pressure that indicated she should turn and go the opposite way down the hall.

"Yes, I'll just go see about Bernadette." She retreated, leaving Tyler to deal with his mother-in law while she fixed every ounce of mental energy on keeping her balance and finding Bernadette's room.

Neither proved very easy, but finally, after a few directions from Mabel and an occasional wobble, Lucky found the pink wallpapered room. The feminine decor went no farther than the walls, however. A double bed draped with a thick orange and white quilt dominated the room and Lucky wished she'd thought to grab sunglasses out of the cab. Maybe she could charge Tight Tush extra for eyestrain.

The thought stayed with her as she scanned the rest of the room. A pair of huge black rubber boots flanked one side of the closet, the soles caked in dried mud. A desk occupied another corner. Schoolbooks lay scattered across the top. Lucky thought she saw beige carpet beneath the mess of clothes on the floor. Overall, the entire room looked as if a tornado had whipped through.

Or the very sulky-looking girl who sprawled on a lime-green beanbag chair, her eyes glued to a handheld Nintendo game. She had dark hair the exact shade as her father's, but hers was slightly longer and pulled into a haphazard ponytail. A bleep sounded and she frowned, her expression exactly the same as one Tyler would have worn. Her features were softer, more delicate, her complexion several shades lighter than her father's, but otherwise the resemblance was eerie.

"Bernadette?"

The girl didn't spare her a glance.

"I'm Luck—retia. Did your father mention me?"

The girl let out a heavy sigh. "The name's Bennie. B-E-N-N-I-E," she spelled. "And you're another one of the agency nannies. A fill-in until the permanent nanny arrives to replace Miss Walker who left unexpectedly. Though I'm not supposed to mention any of that to my grandmother. As far as she's concerned, you're the permanent nanny. Grandmother would have a fit if she thought I'd scared another one away."

So Bennie didn't know about the con-artist nanny. That would make things harder, because she expected Lucky to act like a real nanny. To *be* the nanny.

Lucky cleared her throat and did her best Fran Drescher imitation. "Well, your grandmother's here and your dad wants us front and center."

Bennie shook her head. "You can report for duty. I'm not going anywhere."

"But your grandmother came a long way to see you." Lucky pushed aside some of the clothes covering the bed and sat down. Sighing, she slid her feet free of the heels. Her toes launched into a chorus of "Born Free." "Don't you want to see her?"

"Sure I do, but like I told Dad and Mabel, I'm not wearing that." Bennie stuck her nose up at a white lace dress that lay several feet away.

"That…that's something, all right." It really was a beautiful dress, and that was the trouble. It was too pretty. A hands-off dress, the kind you wore for really special occasions, not the sort of dress you could really breathe in. Lucky was getting claustrophobic just looking at it.

"I want to wear jeans and I don't see why I can't."

"But tonight isn't just any night. Your dad's trying to make a good impression on your grandmother."

Bennie rolled her eyes. "But I look awful in that and it's itchy and Grandmother would have a fit if I started scratching myself at the dinner table. One time I burped and she almost had a heart attack."

Lucky caught a giggle with her hand and pretended to

cough. "Well, can't you just scratch discreetly?" Bennie seemed to give the idea some thought. "I'll make you a deal," Lucky went on, trying to tip the scales in her favor. "When you start to itch, you just wink at me. I'll distract your grandmother and let you get in a few good scratches. She'll never know." When Bennie stayed silent, Lucky added, "Your dad's trying real hard to impress her and he wants us to help him. I'll let you in on a little secret, I haven't gotten all dressed up like this in a long time, myself." Try never. Oh, well, she was fibbing for a good cause. Surely that counted for something.

Bennie gave her a thorough once-over. "You should do it more often. Your hair looks real nice. The clothes, too." Another quick glance and she started to giggle. "But I can tell you aren't used to wearing heels."

Lucky glanced down at her throbbing feet. "Does it really show that much?"

Bennie nodded, suddenly all serious sympathy, and got up to place a hand atop Lucky's. "If you help me scratch, I'll distract Grandmother whenever you have to stand up."

Lucky smiled. "You've got yourself a deal."

WHILE LUCKY WHEELED and dealed with Bennie, Tyler listened to Helen drone on about her newest charity project and kept a watchful eye on the door. Where the hell were they?

"...we're planning a special theme for the event, grandmothers and granddaughters, and it's sure to be one of the biggest galas this season."

"Wonderful," he murmured as Mabel walked in with a tray of canapés.

Helen surveyed the hors d'oeuvres. "My Clara uses artichokes instead of mushrooms."

"Artichokes overwhelm the taste," Mabel declared, despite the warning look Tyler gave her. "Mushrooms bring out the spices used in the bottom layer of homemade relish."

Helen shook her head. "Perhaps that's the way things are

prepared out here, but in Houston we do things a little differently. My chef, Clara, trained at La Dubois in Paris. Did you know that, Tyler?"

"Don't think I've ever heard of it." Tyler didn't miss the flush of anger creeping into Mabel's face. Uh-oh.

"Come now," Helen said, and laughed. "La Dubois is one of the best restaurants in the world. Five-plus stars. Now, now," she added when Mabel's face looked ready to explode. "No one expects five-star cuisine way out here, dear. I'm sure your mushrooms are very...tasty."

"I like mushrooms," Tyler piped in, but it didn't ease the harsh lines around Mabel's mouth. He gave Mabel his biggest smile. "So what's for dinner?"

"Your head on a platter," Mabel whispered as she whisked past him with the platter of canapés.

"I'm afraid I didn't hear her." Helen cast a curious gaze on him. "What did she say?"

"It's a surprise." Tyler poured himself a glass of Scotch and downed it in one quick gulp. "Mabel loves surprises."

"You really shouldn't drink so quickly. It looks positively uncivilized. Speaking of which, where is your father?"

"He had an upset stomach. He'll be having dinner in his room."

"Did he have some of Mabel's canapés?"

"Afraid not. He saved them all for you." Okay, as much as he wanted to please Helen, he had his limits.

"He shouldn't have bothered, but what a...lovely gesture, I suppose. Such a sweet old thing. Do give him my regrets. I was looking forward to seeing the poor man again."

"Rest assured, he's equally heartbroken." Or he would be heartbroken, if he had to sit and listen to Helen all evening. She was too much a reminder of Tyler's mother, and her presence never failed to cause a bout of depression in Ulysses, and an insatiable craving for Maalox.

He motioned to Helen. "Let's go into the dining room."

"Merle's still not here." She glanced at the diamond Rolex

circling her wrist. "If it's a business dinner, he's early, but tack on the word *social,* and he'll be late every time. I should have taken his cellular phone away before I got out of the car. By the way, where is Bernadette?"

"Right here, Grandmother." Bennie appeared in the doorway.

Tyler's gaze moved to the lace-scalloped white dress Bennie wore, the matching quarter-inch pumps. He blinked. His Bennie? Wearing a dress and smiling at the same time?

"Darling!" Helen cried, opening her arms wide. Dutifully, Bennie walked into her grandmother's embrace.

"You got her to put on a dress," Tyler said, sidling up beside Lucky who stood in the doorway, one hand braced on the doorjamb. "I'm impressed."

"Piece of cake." She smiled at Helen who smiled at Bennie, obviously pleased with her granddaughter's wardrobe choice.

"Do you remember the drill?" he asked.

"Wealthy oilman, kids, Scotland…piece of cake."

"Miss Myers," Helen started, but the clatter of dishes from the dining room effectively drowned out the rest of her sentence. Every gaze turned toward the archway.

"Dinner is served," Mabel announced, her face pinched into a frown directed solely at Helen.

"I don't suppose we're having a nice big piece of Bubble Yum?" Lucky whispered, her eyes hopeful as Tyler steered her forward, all the while conscious of Helen's intense gaze.

"Remember the story and I'll buy you an entire case of the stuff," he promised in a low voice. His grip tightened ever so lightly when Lucky snagged her heel on the plush carpet and started to pitch forward.

"What do you think of my dress, Grandmother?" Bennie piped up, effectively distracting Helen while Lucky caught her balance.

"Lovely, dear. Just lovely." Helen followed Bennie, who

twirled toward the dining room. "Wait until you see the outfit I brought for you. It's simply divine."

"What did you do to my daughter?" he whispered to Lucky.

"We have an agreement. She scratches my back and I scratch hers. So to speak." A warm giggle passed her lips.

The sound filtered through Tyler's head, skimming his nerve endings like champagne bubbles tickling his nose. A strange warmth flooded him.

Think cool thoughts, he told himself. Searching for a lost calf during the dead of winter. Plunging into an ice-cold creek after hours of herding cattle.

Try as he might, though, he couldn't summon any goose bumps, or push away the enticing image of Lucky underneath him, soft and warm and open. Especially with her so close.

She was good, all right. A woman who knew how to rope, hog-tie and brand a man without him ever knowing what happened.

"Here." He thrust her into a chair so fast she had to catch the edge of the table to keep from tipping over. He skipped a chair and sat down, ignoring her raised eyebrow. Bennie took her seat opposite Tyler, and Helen sat down beside her.

"Well, it's about time," Helen declared, her gaze darting to the dining-room doorway. "We were about to start dinner without you."

Tyler turned to see his father-in-law, a large man with gray hair and matching eyes, looking impeccable in a charcoal suit.

"Good to see you, Tyler," Merle said, clapping Tyler on the shoulder and giving him a quick handshake before rounding the table to hug his granddaughter and sit on her free side.

"Whatever took you so long—" Helen's sentence drowned in a high-pitched buzz.

"Hold that thought, dear." Merle reached into his coat and pulled out a cellular phone. "Whitman here," he barked into the phone, before mumbling, "Excuse me, I have to take this call."

"So," Helen said as a scowling Mabel started ladling soup into everyone's bowl. "Tell me about yourself, Miss Myers. You're from the Dalton Agency, correct?"

"Yes, she is," Tyler interjected. "She's one of their best. She's been living in Scotland the past few years, caring for the children of a rich Texas oilman."

"Why, I know nearly every oil family in the state. What's his name?"

"Uh, Mel," Lucky stammered, shooting Tyler a panicked look. "I mean, er, Dale. Dale...Stinson. Yes, Dale Stinson."

"Dale Stinson?" Helen asked. "You say he's in oil?"

"Among other things."

"Well, I can't say as I've ever heard of him. Merle—" she turned to her husband "—do you know any Stinsons?"

"Tell him no," Merle grumbled into the phone before throwing Helen a distracted glance. "What, dear?"

"Stinsons. Do you know any Stinsons?" He shook his head and Helen went on, "The name certainly strikes a familiar chord. Tyler, are you acquainted with this Mr. Stinson?"

"Not personally, but I've heard of him. Mr. Stinson is very busy overseas. Scotland is practically his first home."

Helen stared expectantly at Lucky. "What part of Scotland?"

"Glasgow," Tyler fired off before Lucky could open her mouth. "That reminds me, isn't there a display of Scottish armament at the Museum of Fine Arts? Speaking of museums, I'm sure Bennie would love to hear about the new addition to the children's museum."

"Oh, yes. The new wing will be splendid. And with me as chairwoman for the fund-raising gala, it's sure to be *the* event of the season..." Her voice droned on as Lucky turned her attention to the silverware surrounding the bowl of soup in front of her.

Tyler reached for the appropriate utensil and felt Lucky's anxious gaze on him. She followed his every move as he silently coached her through the soup and salad. To her credit, she carried off everything as if she'd been born to it. Tyler actually started to relax. By the time they reached the chicken entrée, he was even enjoying himself. There were worse things than being stared at by an attractive woman. Then the evening took a sharp turn toward Disaster City.

Bernadette, a fidgety audience for her grandmother who talked nonstop about the upcoming fund-raiser, shifted in her chair. Her expression went from attentive to uncomfortable, to desperate. She stared at Lucky. Their gazes met for all of three seconds, then Lucky's fork clattered to the table.

"Those Scottish," Lucky declared in a loud voice that made even Merle pause, cellular phone in hand. "Talk about ingenious. You know, I never knew that mooning was a historical part of battle."

Tyler's jaws locked around a bite of chicken.

"Then there it was on the big screen, Mel Gibson flashing his assets for the entire English army. I realized then why the Scottish really wear those kilts. Definitely a distraction if there's five hundred guys waiting to slice you into mincemeat."

Helen looked horrified.

Tyler swallowed and bolted out of his chair. "If you'll excuse us. I think Miss Myers is having one of her spells."

"Spells?" Lucky asked.

"Hot spells. Where you get dizzy, disoriented, *stupid.*" He muttered the last word for her ears only.

"Oh, yes, yes. One of my spells." She fanned her face dramatically and let him usher her out of her chair.

"You look like you're the one having the spell," Lucky said in a hushed whisper. "You're all red."

"That's because my butt is in the hot seat," he hissed, steering her toward the door. "And you just put me there."

"Oh no," she replied as he whisked her out into the hallway. "I would never do that to you or your butt," she said, her voice filled with conviction. "*Especially* your butt."

6

"LEAVE MY BUTT out of this." Tyler whirled on her.

"You were the one who brought it up. And since you did, I've been meaning to tell you. It's quite impressive."

"What are you? A butt connoisseur?"

"Some women like muscular arms, some like hands, some like chests, I like butts. What's wrong with that?"

"Nothing, except you don't have to go pointing it out to my mother-in-law, who, by the way, is supposed to think you're a high-society nanny."

"So nannies can't like butts?"

"You're insane." His frustrated whisper echoed off the paneled walls. "I say, 'Don't talk. Don't invite questions.' Do you listen? Of course not. Hell, you not only talk, you go ninety to nothing about men showing off their butts and their—"

"Keep your voice down or they'll hear you." Lucky motioned to the partially open door leading to the dining room. The heel of his boot shot out, the door slammed shut and Lucky jumped.

"You deliberately drew attention to yourself when I had her distracted," he hissed, "talking about her fund-raiser."

"You had her looking at Bennie with every other word."

"So?"

"Soooo," she exaggerated the word. "Being a lady isn't all it's cracked up to be. Take me for instance. I'm all decked out in this blouse and skirt, stockings, slip—the whole package, and I look very ladylike, but as for comfort…" She slid her feet free of the killer heels. "These shoes are straight out of an episode of Torture Devices of the Strange and Deranged."

"What do your shoes have to do with the hot topic of butts?"

"Nothing. They're just an example of what we women endure to make you men happy. Which brings me to my point. You wanted Bennie in a dress. She agreed, but there were conditions."

"What conditions?"

"That I would sort of help her out if she needed to scratch. You see, all that lace is very uncomfortable. I know because there was this time in the fifth grade when I got picked to be the fairy princess in the Christmas pageant. Not that I wanted to be the fairy princess. I wanted to be the troll that lived under the bridge. He got to wear a beard and boots and carry this leather scabbard, not that it was real, but it looked real and... Anyway, I was too tall for the troll, so I wound up in lace tights and fairy wings, and I was still too tall. The tights were too small, and every time I moved they slipped lower and the lace rubbed my skin raw."

"Let me get this straight, you launched into a discussion about Mel Gibson's butt and screwed things up with Helen, just so Bernadette could *scratch* herself?"

She nodded and watched him digest the information, his face solemn, his eyes as hard as turquoise chips. Just when the tension was thick enough to smother her, he burst out laughing.

"You're not mad?" she blurted out.

"Why would I be mad?"

"Well, scratching's not very ladylike, and I didn't exactly keep my end of the bargain, but I had to talk fast, and I was nervous." She gave Tyler a wide-eyed look. "What do we do now?"

"*We* don't do anything. I'll head back in there and see if I can patch up any mess you made. And you," he said, glancing at his watch, "are off the hook for now. Dinner is practically finished. I'll just tell Helen the spell got worse and you called it a night."

She took a deep breath. "So it's over."

"*Almost* over," he corrected. "After another quick performance at breakfast, you'll be finished, Helen will be out of here and I'll be off the hook." He passed a hand over his face and she noticed how tired he suddenly looked.

Her heart gave a painful thud.

"I'm really sorry if I messed things up."

"At least it was for a good cause." His fingertips brushed her jaw, straightening the silk collar that had somehow turned up. "But under no circumstances bring up the subject again."

"Deal," she said, hoping her voice sounded even while her senses were spinning. Bouncing. Doing a very fast, furious version of the macarena.

"Thanks for helping Bennie," he said.

"Thank you," she breathed.

"For what?"

For making me feel like Dorothy spinning away into the unknown. For making my heart pound so fast I feel as if I'm having cardiac arrest. For making me feel things I haven't ever felt before. "For not being mad," she finally said. "And for having *the* best pair of buns I've ever seen."

An odd glimmer lit his eyes. "I'm not going near the buns comment, but I'm certainly not angry." He touched her shoulder and trailed his fingertips down her arm. "Though I'm not so sure about mad."

Before she could question him, he pulled his hand away, his fingers skimming the side of one breast in the process.

"Sleep tight." He turned to stride back into the dining room while she stood there, barely breathing, trying to figure out what had just happened between them.

He'd touched her. Not just touched, but *caressed.* Her nipple stood at attention beneath the cream silk blouse and a wave of heat flooded her face.

Not that his touch meant anything. Tyler Grant was a flirt, a lady-killer, a wildcatter, wielding charm and sex appeal like Rambo with an Uzi. A girl had to be careful. She could enjoy the attention, the flirting, the whole seduction game, but she couldn't forget whom she was playing with, no matter how her traitorous hormones tried to claim amnesia.

It was just a game, and Tyler Grant was one smooth player. And for the first time, Lucky was off the bench and smack-dab in the middle of the action.

"CHECKMATE!" Helen cried after the shortest chess game in the history of the world. "Didn't you see me coming, Tyler? Why, even a child wouldn't have made that last move. It played right into my hands." The implications were there, but Helen was too pleased at winning against Tyler, who never lost a chess match, to see it as anything more than a well-deserved victory.

"You must be feeling a little under the weather, son," Merle said, sparing a glance at the chessboard before he resumed his pacing. His steps paused periodically as he dictated into a microcassette recorder.

"Actually, there must be something going around." Tyler patted his middle. "I'm feeling a little queasy. I think I'll look in on Bennie then call it a night."

"But it's only a little after nine," Helen cried. "I was hoping we would have a chance to discuss Bernadette's enrollment at Smithston. I've brought the brochures and an application—"

Tyler interrupted with an exaggerated moan. "Cramp," he croaked in explanation, clutching his middle.

"This isn't one of those spells your nanny had, is it?" Her words dripped sarcasm and Merle patted her shoulder.

"Now, now, dear. The woman couldn't help herself. You heard Tyler. It hits her suddenly. That's understandable with her being so accustomed to the cool Scottish weather. This must be quite a change for her, though I can't say as I've ever heard of a heat allergy."

"I'm sure my cramp had nothing to do with an allergy," Tyler assured them. "Probably something I ate."

"I bet it's the mushrooms," he heard Helen tell Merle after he'd bid them both good-night and started for the hallway. "They're dangerous. Not fit for civilized taste buds."

"You're allergic to mushrooms," Merle said.

"I am not. I have an iron constitution. The Bells don't have allergies, dear. We're all as healthy as horses."

Their voices faded as Tyler headed down the hall, past the kitchen and library. He turned a corner toward Bennie's room.

"I tell you, Ulysses." Mabel's voice carried from his father's partially open bedroom door. "That woman is downright rude. Imagine her criticizing my food. Why, I've won the annual pie competition for the past five years in a row. That woman wouldn't know a frying pan if it jumped out of the cupboard and bit her on the rump. And it wouldn't have a lick of trouble finding its target..."

Tyler rubbed his tired eyes. *It's almost over.* The thought gave him the energy to push open the door to Bennie's room.

She sprawled across the bed on her stomach, her chin propped on one hand as she scanned the pages of *Texas Horse and Trainer*. The package Helen had brought her lay on the floor several feet away.

"Hi, Daddy." She smiled up at him.

"Did you like your new outfit?"

"Ugh, are you kidding? It's white with roses all over it."

"I'm sure it's pretty. Why don't you try it, honey? You might like getting dressed up once in a while."

She gave a heavy sigh. "Okay, maybe I'll try it."

"That's my girl. Lights out in five minutes."

Her mouth dropped open. Before she could get in a word edgewise, he turned and pulled the door closed. Bennie would argue until doomsday if Tyler gave her the chance. And he tried never to do that, especially since she was so effective at wearing him down. When she turned a smile on him, he was a goner. Thankfully, she hadn't figured that out yet. The day she did, he'd be in deep trouble. But he was already in deep trouble, a voice reminded him when he heard a door open, then walked smack-dab into Lucky.

"Oops, I'm sorry," she mumbled, her hands splayed against his chest as she caught herself. "I didn't hear you out here."

"Obviously." His gaze scanned her rumpled T-shirt and bare legs. Legs that went on forever. Long and tanned and...

Tyler swallowed and forced his attention back to her face. "Do you always walk around half-dressed?"

"I'm not half-dressed. Girls at the beach show ten times more than I'm showing, and I didn't think it would matter what I was wearing in the privacy of my room."

"You aren't in the privacy of your room. You're out in the hallway." His gaze lowered of its own accord, and he saw the goose bumps rise on her tanned skin. His fingers itched to reach out and ease her sudden chill.

Chill? How could she be cold? He was burning up. Hot, and getting hotter by the millisecond.

"I was just going to tiptoe to Bennie's room and say good-night," she told him. "I didn't expect to find you lurking in the hallway."

"I wasn't lurking. I was saying good-night myself."

"Good night then," she said, but before she could dart past him, he felt himself leaning toward her.

"Yes, it is a good night. A very good night..." He pressed against her, his chest brushing the tips of her breasts. A subtle touch, but it was still enough to send a jagged bolt of lightning down his spine, straight to his groin.

She looked startled for a quick moment, then her gaze brightened with wonder. It was the cookie look all over again, and the realization sent another jolt through him.

"I...I know this is harmless flirting and all," she stammered. "But I don't think this is really safe..."

He watched her form the words, warn him about Helen and

why their current stance was too provocative. But what she was saying didn't really register. The only thing that stuck was the way she moved her lips. Full, soft lips he wanted so much to taste, needed to taste.

"I really want to kiss you," he told her.

"Me? Really—"

Then his mouth covered hers. He tasted her, nibbled the fullness of her bottom lip while she stood stiff as a board. Then she opened her lips on a sigh and her moment of surprise passed. His tongue tangled with hers, stroking, coaxing, and sensation skimmed down his spine, clear to his toes.

It was unlike anything he'd ever felt before, anything he should feel with this woman. There was nothing particularly special about her. Sure she was attractive, and she tasted really good... To hell with good. She was intoxicating, mesmerizing. *Of course, Sherlock.* She knew exactly what she was doing. She'd probably practiced this innocent-hungry thing on some other poor sap who'd fallen hook, line and sinker. But not Tyler. He wasn't some gullible, hot-for-anything-in-a-skirt guy. No way. Not him.

He deepened the kiss, drinking in her sweetness, and she melted against him. She was just so...innocent. So...hungry. And she wasn't even wearing a skirt. Right. Tell that to the judge, sucker.

From far away he heard the slam of a door, the low murmur of voices and he forced himself away from her.

"Wow," she said, her eyes closed, her head resting against the wall as if she didn't have the energy to hold it up. "That was something."

Something, all right. But what?

Nothing, he told himself as he spun on his heel and walked away from her. It was just chemistry between them. She was a mistress of seduction with all that wide-eyed charm, and he was just a lowly guy. A starving dog in the face of a juicy T-bone.

Only for a little while. Thankfully, she would be gone tomorrow. He focused on that thought and strode outside to the barn. Some neighboring kids had been out joyriding on their daddy's tractor and had plowed down a stretch of fence in the north pasture earlier that day. The last thing he wanted was to be out fixing fences, but he knew he didn't stand a chance of sleeping and with cattle grazing that pastureland he had to get the barbed wire back up.

Fifteen minutes later, Tyler urged his horse forward, across the dark pasture. He reached the broken fence and went to work stretching the loose wire and stapling it tight. Even with the ranch smaller than Tyler remembered, there was always work to do.

Guilt shot through him. At one time this ranch had rivaled its namesake from the movie *Giant*, the half-million-acre spread dominated by Rock Hudson and Elizabeth Taylor. But no more. The ranch had dwindled, a parcel of land sold here and there, until his father's Reata was just a shadow of what it had once been, the herd nearly sold off.

Tyler was doing his damnedest to change that. In less than two months since his return, he'd managed to track down several of the people who'd bought a piece of his father's land. He'd purchased every last acre back, all except for a few acres here and there. He was so very close to seeing Reata exactly the way it had been before he'd left sixteen years ago. Before he'd broken his father's heart by walking away.

But past regrets were just that. Past. He was home, he was making up for lost time, reclaiming Reata and increasing the size of the herd. Things were falling into place. Now if he could just send Helen packing, her mind at ease that her granddaughter was becoming every bit the lady her daughter had been, he'd be sitting pretty.

CAFFEINE. She needed caffeine.

Lucky stumbled toward the kitchen the next morning, her eyes blurry, her neck stiff and her legs wobbly from a restless night in an unfamiliar bed. And let's not forget the dreams.

The sort that made your cheeks burn and your body crave a cold shower.

But of course, the shower hadn't helped a bit. Ah, but the caffeine. A little coffee, a diet soda, a piece of chocolate cake—the desperate woman's cure-all.

She adjusted the too-tight waistband of the black slacks she'd found in the guest room and promised herself she'd start a diet the minute she got home. Exercise, her conscience screamed, but she stifled the voice before it could summon any guilt. Lucky had long ago convinced herself that the walk to the refrigerator counted as exercise.

She peeked into the kitchen to make sure the coast was clear. Although she was dressed like Nanny of the Year, she was in no hurry to run into anyone. She couldn't think, talk, even smile until she'd revved up her system.

"Bad night?" Tyler's voice sounded behind her and she jumped.

"Geez, don't do that. You scared me."

"*I* scared *you?*" His critical gaze fixed on her and he fingered a wayward strand of hair that had slipped loose from the hairband she'd borrowed from Bennie. "I take it you're not a morning person?"

"I'm fine in the mornings," she grumpily replied. "It's the middle of the night I have trouble with."

"It's 6:00 a.m."

"My point exactly. It's still dark out. Morning doesn't really start for at least another two hours."

"For you. Here we're up at five."

"Ugh," she said, slumping against the wall, wishing he wasn't standing so close and her head wasn't pounding so hard. Or was that her heart? It couldn't be her heart. Not this early. Not without a shot of caffeine.

"Go on back to your room and finish getting dressed," he said. "I'll have Mabel bring you a cup of coffee."

"I am finished," she said defensively, tucking the traitorous strand of hair behind one ear.

"Not your hair. Your shirt is on backward."

"It is not." She glanced down at the simple crew-neck pull-over she'd found hanging in the closet. "How can you tell? It looks exactly the same from both sides."

"They don't put tags on both sides," he said, fingering the white flag peeking up at her collar. One fingertip brushed the pulse beat at the base of her neck and her breath caught.

"Uh-oh." She lifted her hand to shove the stubborn tag back beneath the neckline. "I could have sworn I had it right."

"These things can be tricky." He watched her fidget with the tag. She shoved it down, and it found its way back up again.

"Blast it," she muttered.

"Blast what?" came a woman's voice.

Lucky's gaze swiveled back toward the kitchen to see Mabel standing in the doorway, a basket of fresh eggs in her hands.

"Nothing," Tyler said, grabbing the tag and tearing it free.

"Thank you," Lucky breathed. The smile he gave her warmed her insides better than hot cocoa on the coldest morning.

"What are we blasting?" A jug of milk in her hands, Bennie followed Mabel inside, pausing to wipe her feet when the older woman frowned at her.

"I don't want any traces of that barn on my clean floor."

"Yes, ma'am," Bennie said. "Look, Daddy. We milked Betty Lou. Mabel's going to make pancakes and sausage for breakfast and fresh whipped cream from this milk." Bennie set the pitcher down on the counter. Picking up a half-empty glass of juice, she took a huge gulp.

"Shouldn't you be wearing something else?" Tyler asked her, his gaze going from her plain blue T-shirt, down past her blue jeans and sneakers, then back up again. "Like a dress."

"But Daddy—"

"You know your grandmother will be upset if she sees you like that. Put on that outfit she brought you last night, the one with the pink flower things on it." When Bennie turned a horrified expression on him, he added, "Please, honey. You'll look really pretty."

"Of course she will," Helen declared, walking into the kitchen. She wore an apricot-colored silk blouse and slacks, her makeup and hair perfect, as if she'd just walked out of a salon. Her cool eyes zeroed in on Lucky who busied herself drinking orange juice. "You look positively wretched."

The juice stuck in Lucky's throat. Wretched? Tired, maybe, out of sorts, even under the weather, but *wretched?* Definitely too harsh a word, even for somebody who'd put on her shirt backward. "Actually, I'm feeling much better."

Helen's eyes narrowed slightly. "Good, then you can join me. We didn't get much of a chance to chat last night."

"I'm sure Miss Myers would rather retire to her room. She's still a little ill." Tyler's gaze riveted on her. "Aren't you?"

"Come now, Tyler. If the girl says she's feeling better, then I'm sure she's feeling better, no matter how she looks." Helen sat down at the breakfast table and patted the seat next to her. "Come and have a seat, Miss Myers. I won't bite you."

Lucky started to ask Helen if she would be willing to put that in writing, but instead of her own voice, she heard Tyler's.

"I'm sure Miss Myers would love to visit, but she needs to rest. I want her in top form for Bernadette."

At the mention of her granddaughter, Helen gave Lucky another thorough once-over. "She does look a little pale. And those clothes…"

"I'm feeling fine," Lucky heard herself say a second before she felt Tyler's hand on her arm.

"The medicine," he declared, his grip warning her not to say any more. "I think she took a little too much for her heat allergy and now everything's a little disorganized upstairs."

"I haven't taken anything—" His fingers tightened and the words stalled in her throat. "Actually, I could lie down a few minutes. Oh, my pounding head,'' she added for good measure.

"Medicine." Helen looked thoughtful. "Well, it's a relief to know she doesn't behave this way on a regular basis. I would hate to think this is the sort of woman you hired to teach my granddaughter how to conduct herself like a proper young lady."

"I don't need anyone to teach me anything," Bennie chimed in, only to have Tyler cut her off.

"Rest assured, Miss Myers is the epitome of grace and elegance. This is simply a bad day for her."

"And is this one of your bad days, as well?" Helen gave him a pointed stare. "You look dreadful, Tyler. In fact, I don't think I've ever seen you quite so *rough*-looking." She sniffed. "And that smell. What have you been doing?"

"It's called work," he replied, his voice calm and even, though Lucky could feel the tension in his body, his fingers still firm on her arm. "Why don't you visit with Bernadette while I help Miss Myers back to her room and get cleaned up?"

"A lovely idea," Helen said. "Miss Myers and I can chat later when she's feeling better. A long chat, after breakfast."

"Not enough time, I'm afraid." Tyler did his best to look regretful, but Lucky could see the relief dancing in his eyes. "If you and Merle are going to make San Antonio by nine, you'll have to hit the road in the next half hour."

"There's been a change of plans. Merle had urgent premeeting business." Helen stared pointedly at the pitcher of juice, then at Mabel who looked as if she'd rather eat nails than pour the woman a drop. "He left an hour ago."

"*Left?* But y-you're still here."

"Of course I am, Tyler. One evening is so little time. I thought I would just stay and get reacquainted while Merle went on without me. I'm staying two weeks." She smiled and clasped Bennie's hand. "Two wonderful weeks to visit with my granddaughter and—'' she shifted her attention to Lucky "—get to know the woman you've hired to care for her.''

Lucky forced a swallow and turned her gaze to the man with the iron grip on her elbow.

And for the first time since she'd met him, Lucky saw Tyler Grant completely and utterly speechless.

7

"YOU'RE NOT GOING to throw up, are you?" Lucky watched Tyler pace the length of the library, a strange expression on his face.

"*Staying,*" he muttered. "She's staying." He raked tense fingers through his hair. "For two weeks. *Two* weeks." He shot her an incredulous glance and kept pacing, his complexion visibly paler. He was upset, really upset, and she had the insane urge to cross the room and wrap her arms around him.

It was definitely too early in the morning.

"I'll just go back to my room and pack," she told him. "That way, if you really want to toss your cookies, you don't have to worry about being unmacho in front of me. I was hoping to make it home before the lunch-hour traffic. It's really heavy near the airport on Saturday—"

"You can't leave." He turned in her direction. "She's staying for two weeks."

"I understand that." He'd gone off the deep end. She could see the desperation in his eyes and it did funny things to her. She could feel the sympathy churning inside her, spreading, swamping her common sense.

"No," she blurted out as he advanced.

"No what?"

"No to whatever you're thinking."

"You can't leave. Please, Lucky. It's just two weeks."

"I can't abandon my life for two weeks."

"Not abandon. Just take a little vacation. You don't have a husband waiting at home, no kids."

"But I've got my granny. I visit every Monday. What will she say when I don't show up?"

"I don't know. What?"

She opened her mouth, but the words stalled on her lips. What would Granny say? Probably nothing. With Alzheimer's, half the time she didn't recognize Lucky. She simply sat out in the garden, picking flowers. She loved the nursing-home flowers.

The thousand-dollar-a-month nursing home that Lucky could barely afford. Forget afford. She was two months behind, her tuition money hanging in the balance, and she was desperate. As desperate as Tight Tush staring at her with his deep blue eyes.

"You really think we can pull this off for two weeks?"

"I'll help you, teach you everything you need to know. It won't be easy, but you can do it."

You can do it. For those few moments as he stared at her, she actually did feel like she could. Funny how blind faith could pump up your ego and make you contemplate the impossible.

She shook her head. "I know you're in a tough situation, but I can't lose two weeks of work."

"I'll pay you," he said. "Another thousand. That makes two thousand dollars for two weeks of your time."

She shook her head. "I'm already getting a thousand for last night, so technically it would only be one thousand dollars for two weeks of my time. I want two thousand for two weeks, plus last night's money."

"*Three* thousand dollars? For pretending to be my nanny? I could get a real one for less than that."

"Yes, but I'm already here, and you're asking a lot. You want me to risk my life way out here for peanuts? No way."

"Risk your life?"

"Your father nearly shot me yesterday."

"I took his gun away, so there's no risk. Two thousand," he insisted. "Total. That's my offer. Take it or leave it."

"You must not be a morning person, either."

"What does that mean?"

"You're not thinking clearly, otherwise, you would realize what a terrible mistake you're making. Helen already thinks I'm the governess, and you would have a lot of explaining to do if I up and left and you had to call the agency again."

He sighed. "Now I do feel like throwing up."

She smiled. "Agree to my terms and the urge will pass."

"Three thousand dollars." He ran a hand over his tired face. "I must be out of my mind."

"Three thousand, plus the eighty-dollar cab fare your nanny stiffed me for. *And* you promise to get rid of any and all firearms in the house."

He nodded. "All right, three thousand and eighty dollars, and the guns are history." His gaze zeroed in on her again. "But remember. You do everything I say, when I say it, and overall, do your best to avoid Helen. Got it?"

"I'll try." Doubt crept in and took a few bites out of Lucky's ego. "Do you really think I can pull this off?"

"You have to. Now stay in your room while I shower and change. I'll meet you back here in half an hour, after I have a sit-down with Bennie and tell her your post is going to take a little longer to fill, so you'll be staying for a few weeks."

"She's really great," Lucky said.

For a split second, his harsh expression eased and a smile tugged at his lips. "I know, that's why I can't let this little setback mess everything up. Bennie is the one thing I've done right in my life."

"Oh, I'd be willing to bet you've done more than just one, Tyler Grant." That kiss, for instance. *Ooo, boy.*

She turned and left, her heart pounding double time. Mabel must have put something in the orange juice because Lucky was usually comatose until 8:00 a.m.

WHAT THE HELL was he doing?

The thought flashed in his mind as he watched her leave

the room, her hips molded beneath the clinging black slacks.

Control, he told himself. She was his employee, he was her employer, and despite the sparks between them, she wasn't his type. When, *if* he ever settled down again, it would have to be with someone like Nan. Someone sophisticated, wealthy, refined. Helen's idea of an appropriate wife.

Lucky was completely off limits. He would coach her and pass her off as the best nanny this side of the Rio Grande. Nothing more. Period.

"Lucky's staying?" Bennie said when Tyler told her the news. Where he'd expected his daughter to turn sulky, accusing eyes on him, she actually smiled.

"It's Miss Myers to you, and it's only for two weeks," Tyler told her. "Until the agency can send a capable replacement."

"Until Grandmother leaves," Bennie chimed in.

"Pure coincidence." Tyler averted his gaze. He couldn't fill Bennie in on the details about the theft and Lucky's true identity. She might slip up and spill the news to Helen. "Miss Myers is very kind to have agreed to stay and help us, so I want you to cooperate and be nice, is that clear?"

"Since when am I not nice, Daddy?"

Tyler gave her a knowing look. "You want the full list?"

Bennie turned red and shook her head. "I'll behave. I'll act like the perfect lady." She gave him a kiss and left.

Lucky joined him in the library a little while later. She'd turned her shirt around, the material molding to her perfect breasts the way the slacks clung to her hips. The clothes were a little too small to look elegant. Inviting, yes. Elegant?

Forget inviting. He needed elegant.

"If you're going to pull this off for two weeks, then we have to prepare. There are certain things Helen will expect you to know. Proper etiquette, culture, who's who in Houston—things like that. We'll start tonight."

"Start what?"

"Lessons," he said, pulling a few leather volumes from the shelves. "Here," he said, handing her the books. "Start reading these."

"*Wine-tasting Made Easy* and *What Not to Say at the Dinner Table.* You're kidding, right?"

He shook his head. "The Dalton Agency doesn't peddle your average nanny/baby-sitter. We're talking educated, sophisticated women. Dalton nannies are trained for the wealthiest families."

"Obviously." Her gaze dropped to the books in her hands. "Gifts from your mother-in-law?"

"Actually, they were my mother's," he said, wondering why he didn't just keep his trap shut. Her gaze lifted, connected with his. That's why. She had eyes that begged him to talk, to pour out his soul. Damn, she was good.

"Trying to better herself?" Lucky asked.

"Trying to better the rest of us," he replied.

"So she didn't go for the rugged-cowboy type?"

He shook his head. "She liked the three-piece suit, pocket-full-of-money type that doesn't sweat or get his hands dirty."

She smiled, her eyes crinkling at the corners, sparkling with honesty and something else. "Well, there's nothing wrong with a little dirt and sweat. It builds character, or that's what my daddy always said. So where is your mother now?"

"She and my dad divorced when I was sixteen. She left and I went to live with her."

"You two must have been close."

Tyler sighed. "There was no being close to my mother, though I tried. I went to the right schools, had the right friends, wore the right clothes, even married the right woman according to my mother's standards. Nannette, Bennie's mom, was as blue-blooded as they come. She was perfect. Beautiful, smart, a product of good breeding and heir to one of the oldest fortunes in Houston."

"Did you love her?"

"You cut right to the chase, don't you?"

She smiled. "I've always been very straightforward. So answer the question. Did you?"

"We weren't *in* love, if that's what you mean. I loved the idea that my mother was so taken with her, and she liked the idea of dating someone her parents didn't approve of."

"You? But you're smart and handsome and—"

"I'm the son of a lowly rancher," he corrected, unable to stifle a surge of pleasure at her quick defense. "My father is self-made. His father was a sharecropper. Peasant stock compared to royalty."

"Nonsense, people are people. We all put our pants on one leg at a time. So you do it in a fifty-room mansion in River Oaks, while I'm in a one-room efficiency on the south side. We're still doing the same thing."

It sounded so simple—too simple to someone who'd spent his life trying to measure up, and too close to the truth. He pulled another volume from the shelf and handed it to her.

She smiled and clasped the books to her chest. "I'm not making any promises. I'm about as peasant as they come, but I'll do my best."

"Fair enough. Just read as much as you can, as fast as you can today, and tonight you and I will meet for a crash course in the fine art of being a Dalton nanny."

Meanwhile, Tyler was going to see what he could do to keep Helen preoccupied for the next two weeks. Right after he tortured himself with another cold shower and gave his libido a good lecture on how to control itself. And his heart. Definitely his heart, he decided when she turned another smile on him. Two weeks.

What the hell had he done?

"DON'T YOU WORRY about a thing. Between me, Buster and the boys, we got your granny covered."

"And tell everybody I'm sorry I have to miss Saturday's game. We're bowling the Quickie Cab Iguanas and I know the guys are nervous."

"About bowling against a bunch of lizards? They'll be fine without you and I'll give 'em your apologies personally."

"Thanks, Stella. You're a lifesaver."

"No need to thank me. Just take care of yourself, and make sure this guy's on the up-and-up."

"Oh, he's legitimate, all right. He gave me part of the money as a down payment, and he seems like a decent guy."

"Don't let him fool you. He's still a man," Stella declared, "and they're all predators, every last one of them. They'll eat you alive at the first sign of weakness."

"I should be so lucky. Of all the things I've ever been afraid of, being eaten alive by a good-looking cowboy has never been one of them."

"Men don't care about looks. As long as you're breathing and you've got double X chromosomes, you're fair prey."

Lucky wasn't in total agreement. Experience had taught her that it took a little more than simply being the correct sex to attract a man, any man, and to catch a guy like Tyler... The task was so daunting she didn't even want to think about it.

For a good-looking man of means like Tyler, a woman would have to have the entire thing going on: great body, great face, an abundance of feminine assets and a mind. One who could read several books in a single afternoon and look dynamite doing it.

Lucky had the mind, but it was all wrapped up in the wrong package. No pretty-colored paper or great big bow. She was more the plain brown wrapping-paper type, with plenty of strapping tape and a warning that read Tampering With Mail Is A Federal Offense. Violators Will Be Prosecuted.

"Don't underestimate him just because he's nice," Stella cautioned. "You're a good girl, easy pickings for a lonely man out there in the middle of nowhere."

Don't I wish, Lucky added silently. "He's definitely not interested, but thanks for the advice."

They talked a minute more while Lucky promised to take care and guard her innocence. Then she hung up and sat down at Tyler's desk to cram for a few more minutes before he arrived for their first nightly lesson.

She tried to concentrate, but talking with Stella had stirred Tyler's image. And sitting in his chair, the scent of leather and male surrounding her, didn't help matters.

Bolting to her feet, she walked over to the broken movie projector. She busied herself putting the pieces that didn't require a screwdriver back together. Still, the task wasn't distracting enough.

Her nerves tingled as she remembered Tyler's soft but firm touch against her breast. Okay, so he was interested, despite what she'd told Stella. But only because Lucky was the only available female for miles.

She was practice. A convenient substitute for some gorgeous, well-endowed socialite. One who didn't put on her shirt backward and could tap-dance "Yankee Doodle" in four-inch stiletto heels without missing a step.

The realization gave her an ill feeling inside, but she forced it away. Forget the whys. Tyler was directing some attention toward her and she was determined to make the most of it. To flirt back and sharpen her own skills so when she returned to Houston, she could do some serious manhunting, she reminded herself.

"That projector is a lost cause," Tyler said, leaning against the doorjamb.

"Nothing is a lost cause." She fit another piece into place then rubbed her hands together. "You haven't seen me with a screwdriver and a wrench."

"You'll have to settle for a fork and a knife." He motioned her to follow him. "Let's go."

"What do you mean and where are we going?"

"Helen's taking a bubble bath, so we're taking advantage of the time. Nanny lesson number one, you can't stare at me all through dinner." He led her into the dining room where she found two complete plate settings with enough silver to kill a dozen werewolves. "There's a reason and a purpose for every fork, knife and spoon," he said.

"But I've been reading all day about wine-tasting."

"That'll come later. This is the most urgent. This and your appearance." His gaze traveled over her face. "Didn't Earline show you any makeup techniques?"

"I like the natural look." Liar. She'd tried for half an hour to duplicate Earline's eye-makeup technique, and had wound up looking like a circus clown. "I think I might need an extra lesson. I've never really been into makeup. It's hard work."

"Mabel can help you. But first things first." He indicated the lavishly laid table.

They started with napkins—the hows, whens and wheres of using them. Then Tyler went through a detailed description of each piece of silverware, and an hour later, Lucky had the headache of her life.

"You're not paying me enough for this." She stifled a yawn. "It's after ten on a Saturday night. I should be getting double-time."

"Think of this as a bonus, not work. You'll be wiser, more socially acceptable. Don't you want to improve yourself? Be a more well-rounded woman?"

Woman. He certainly had a way with words. And gazes. Hungry gazes. Yes, he had the hunger part down pat.

And as for well-rounded... Well, she really wouldn't mind a certain duo being better rounded.

"Okay, so maybe it isn't so bad that I'm learning this stuff." She chewed her bottom lip, a habit she'd picked up over the past twenty-four hours while she was on a gum fast, and studied the place setting. Carefully, she picked up each utensil and repeated what he'd told her. "And bottom line," she finished, "you start at the outside and work your way in."

"Good." The smile he gave her was more than good. It was great, and worth the heavy-metal drum solo beating inside her head. Definitely worth it.

"You know, I've been meaning to ask you," Lucky began.

"Yes?"

"How did you learn to kiss so good? I mean, I'd like to learn, and if there's a school that produces great kissers, I'd be really interested in enrolling."

He stared at her incredulously. "You want to learn how to kiss? You have to be kidding? That kiss..." He shook his head. "I think you've got kissing down pat."

"Me? Really?" She brightened. "You think I'm a good kisser? Why? What was it I did? I need specifics."

"Are you serious? You're serious." He shook his head. "Look, Lucky." He took a deep breath and she saw the muscles in his arms tighten. "That kiss last night... It shouldn't have happened. You and I have to work together. I'm your boss and you're my nanny. Besides that, we're worlds apart and I don't have room in my life for a woman. I've got my daughter to think of, and this ranch and my father... Aw, hell." He leaned forward and captured her lips with his.

Before Lucky knew what was happening, she was in his arms, sitting on his lap, caught in a deep, urgent kiss that sent her senses reeling. Geez, he had great lips. Ah, and a wonderful tongue. He stroked and coaxed and took her breath away, and though she'd promised herself to stay alert and note every nuance for future reference, she couldn't think, much less document Tyler's incredible technique.

He swept her away with his mouth, his hands. His fingers stroked the length of her spine, fitting her against him. Soft female curves to hard male muscle. He felt wonderful. Strong. Hard...

"Tyler, boy, is that you?"

Lucky and Tyler jerked apart at the sound of Ulysses's voice. Lucky scrambled from Tyler's lap, wiping at her lips, her gaze fixed on tall, dark and gorgeous Tyler Grant. He looked stunned, shocked at what had just happened.

"Son?" Tyler's father stood in the doorway, wearing his bathrobe. The bandages were off now, both eyes red and nearly swollen shut. "I can't see a dadblasted thing." Ulysses groped his way into the room and sank into a chair. "Those damn city doctors."

Lucky took deep breaths and tried not to look at Tyler. Not with his father right there.

"Dad, the doctor said to relax. It'll take a few more days for the swelling to subside and for your eyes to adjust to the light. Then, hopefully, your vision will start to return to normal."

"Normal? Hell, I'd be happy with shapes, a few splotches of bright light—somethin' to show me the dadburned surgery actually worked!" He waved his hands in front of him. "You don't know what it's like, boy. A man like me's used to fendin' for himself. It ain't natural for me to be stumblin' around." He felt on the table next to him and grabbed a bowl of potpourri. "So this is where I left my popcorn." Ulysses scooped a handful and prepared to shove it into his mouth.

"Dad!" Tyler grabbed his father's hand.

"What? Now I can't have popcorn? You been talkin' to that doctor about my dadburned cholesterol level again?"

"Dad, this isn't popcorn."

"'Course it is." He tugged at the bowl, but Tyler was stronger. He placed the bowl out of Ulysses's reach.

"Come on, Dad. It's late. Let me help you back to bed."

"I've been in that bed for hours, boy. My back's aching. 'Sides, I could use a little snack. What in blue blazes are you doing?"

"Having a…um, a talk with Miss Myers. She'll be replacing—"

"That dadburned thief! Hot damn, boy, didn't you learn your lesson? You can't trust women like her."

"Ulysses, here you are." Mabel came up behind Tyler's father. "I've been looking all over for you. Come on out to the kitchen and I'll fix you a sandwich."

The old man patted Mabel's hand. "With the little pickles?"

"A whole jar of them," she assured him.

"Lock up your personals, son," Ulysses muttered as he let Mabel help him up and usher him toward the door. "And watch your back."

Lucky shook her head as Ulysses and Mabel made their way down the hall. "Your father doesn't exactly like me."

"It isn't you. It's your type."

"He doesn't like cabdrivers?"

"No, he doesn't like the type of woman he thinks you are— a fortune hunter, just like the nanny who ripped me off. Dad doesn't take too kindly to women only interested in a man's money, whether she wants to marry him or rip him off, or both. Give him a few days and I'm sure he'll mellow."

"And if he doesn't?"

Tyler smiled. "I'll give Hank a call and we'll borrow his bulletproof vest."

8

"I SEE YOU'RE FEELING better today." Helen's gaze roved over Lucky when she arrived for breakfast the following morning.

"A good night's sleep will do wonders." Tyler followed her, looking refreshed and sexy and too damned wide-awake in a red plaid shirt and faded jeans, his damp hair looking deliciously messy.

"Actually, I do feel better." Lucky ignored the urge to touch one damp tendril near his freshly shaven jaw. Instead, she slid into the seat next to Bennie.

"I thought," Tyler said to Helen as he poured syrup onto his pancakes, "we'd take a little look around the ranch after breakfast. Jed is covering for me this morning, so I've got a few hours. How does that sound?"

"Stimulating, dear, but I'm afraid I have other plans." Her gaze locked with Lucky's. "Miss Myers and I have a date to get to know each other better. Did you know that Bernadette will be the fifth-generation Bell to attend Smithston?"

"That little filly isn't a Bell, she's a Grant," Tyler's father said as he felt his way, with Mabel's assistance, to his seat. "And she's staying right here. This is her home."

"*Your* home." Helen turned to Bennie who was busy slathering her pancakes in butter-pecan syrup. "Dear, that's terrible for your heart and your hips."

"I don't have any hips."

"Keep eating this figure-poisoning food and you'll have more than one pair, I guarantee it. Isn't that right, Miss Myers?"

"Not necessarily," Lucky replied. "It's all a matter of metabolism."

"Nonsense." Helen placed the syrup out of Bennie's reach.

"It's a proven scientific fact. I picked up this doctor once—er, met this doctor once, a friend of Mr. Stinson's...a Scottish friend. Anyhow, he'd done a huge amount of research on the subject. Metabolism is everything."

"Perhaps that's true," Helen said, "but there's no way for Bernadette to know what sort of metabolism she has without eating like a horse and seeing where the pounds do or do not accumulate. And if they do accumulate somewhere, primarily the hips, darling, because Merle's family is definitely a hip family, then it's virtually too late to do anything about it." She patted Bennie's hand. "You don't want to be a fat debutante, dear."

"If Grandfather comes from a big-hip family, what do you come from?" Bennie asked around a syrup-drenched pancake.

"A big-mouth family," Ulysses piped in. Tyler nearly choked on his pancakes. Bernadette giggled and Lucky fought to keep from smiling.

"I see you're feeling better, too," Helen told Ulysses.

"Never felt better in my life...er, that is, if my dadburned eyes weren't giving me so much trouble." He blinked the dadburned eyes in question, still red and swollen to little more than slits. "It's a good thing Tyler came home. I'd be lost without the boy."

"I'm sure you could make do just fine with a hired hand."

Ulysses poured syrup over his pancakes. "I could make do just fine if you minded your own business."

"Well, I never..."

"Ain't that the truth," Ulysses grumbled.

"Why, you...you insulting old goat! You make it impossible to carry on a civil conversation."

"Ain't nothin' civil about a stuck-up city gal buttin' into my business."

"Neanderthal," Helen huffed.

"Fund-raisin' fruitcake."

"Stubborn peasant."

"Rich bi—"

"Enough!" Tyler took a deep breath and glared at Ulysses. "Dad, you promised to be nice and this isn't the sort of conversation Bernadette needs to hear." He turned to his mother-in-law. "This…petty name-calling is beneath you, Helen."

Helen, as graceful as ever, sniffed and adjusted her napkin. "Of course, dear, it's just that he…he's so infuriating."

"And she sticks in my craw, boy."

"I don't stick anywhere on your person, least of all your craw. Whatever that is."

"What's a craw, Granddaddy?" Bennie stared hopefully at Ulysses.

"Well, darlin', you see, it's—"

"Not a fit topic for a young lady to be discussing at Sunday morning breakfast," Tyler cut in. "Can we eat, please?"

Ulysses shrugged. "Ask her. She's the one from the big-mouth family."

"That's big hip, Granddaddy," Bennie corrected.

"That's Merle's family." Helen frowned. "And for everyone's information, there are absolutely no ill traits in my family. The Bells are a result of good, pure breeding for over six generations, clear back to English royalty."

"I don't know, Helen." Ulysses wiped a dribble of syrup at the corner of his mouth. "Last I remember, you had a little extra baggage hangin' around them hips of yours."

"Where's my butter knife?" Helen growled. "I'll show you extra baggage, you—"

Ulysses threw down his napkin and staggered to his feet. "Get my shotgun, boy, and let's put the old girl out of her misery!"

"Old girl?" Helen was on her feet, hands on hips, glaring.

"Call 'em like I see 'em."

"And you can't see an inch in front of your face."

"This round's over," Tyler announced. "Everyone back to

their corners." Helen sat down, and Ulysses excused himself and let Mabel help him back to his room.

Lucky couldn't help staring. Angry and frustrated, Tyler still looked good. So tall and muscular and delicious she was ready to chuck the pancakes and have him for breakfast, or lunch, or dinner.

He was every bit the cowboy this morning, with faded jeans that had been washed so many times they looked nearly white. They molded to the lean length of his legs. Scuffed brown boots peeked from the frayed hem. His shirt hugged his shoulders, the sleeves rolled up to reveal tanned forearms sprinkled with dark hair. He wasn't wearing his faded cowboy hat, but Lucky could picture it on his head, shielding his blue eyes and shadowed jaw.

She sighed, her lips still tingling from last night's kiss.

"Are you feeling okay?" Tyler's voice penetrated her thoughts and she sat up straighter. "I know all this carrying on so early is upsetting."

"I'm fine."

"Because you look a little...peaked," he finally said, his eyes assessing her flaming cheeks.

"I feel great." She ate another forkful of pancakes and Tyler turned to Helen.

"Are you sure you wouldn't like to see the rest of Reata?"

"And miss my talk with Miss Myers? Not on your life, Tyler. You run along and do whatever it is you do around here."

"Math right after breakfast," Tyler told Bennie.

"But it's Sunday—"

"And you still haven't finished your lesson from Friday."

"But I want Grandmother to teach me how to fight like she did with Granddaddy."

"Bennie, honey, fighting's not very ladylike," Tyler said.

"That's right." Helen patted her granddaughter's hand. "Ladies disagree, they don't fight."

"Then can I learn how to disagree?" She cast hopeful eyes at Tyler.

"Math," he said, but despite his I-ain't-taking-no-bull expression, there was a softness in his eyes. "Then practice your piano." Bennie made a face and Tyler winked before striding out of the dining room. A few minutes later, Bennie ate the last of her pancakes, and Lucky was left to face the Big Bad Mother-in-law on her own.

"So," Helen declared. "What do you say we find someplace more comfortable and have our little talk?"

"I—"

"Excuse me," Mabel said, appearing in the doorway. She gestured toward Helen. "You've got a phone call. They said something about the Ritz-Carlton withdrawing their offer for your fund-raiser or something like that."

"Oh no." Helen jumped up and rushed out before Lucky could swallow the last of her food.

Mabel moved forward and started clearing away the breakfast dishes. "My advice is to get while the getting is good."

"I'm out of here." Lucky got to her feet, hightailed it through the kitchen and out the back door. Outside was better. Plenty of places to hide from Helen if the need arose.

"You're still in one piece. I guess Helen didn't get much of a chance to talk." Tyler's voice drew her around the side of the house. He stood in front of the barn, saddling the beautiful black horse she'd seen him riding down by the river. "Let me guess, she's on the phone about her gala."

"Good guess."

He gave her a slow smile and Lucky knew there was no guessing involved. Somehow he was behind the sudden fund-raiser upset. Good-looking and clever. She was in deep trouble.

"It could take a while," he went on. "Once she starts in with her high-society friends, she can talk for hours, and this latest setback should keep her busy for a long time." He fastened a strap, gripped the saddle horn and swung himself onto the horse.

"Where are you going?"

"I've got work to do."

"But you can't just leave me here to twiddle my thumbs. What am I supposed to do for the next few hours?"

"Sneak back into your room and read the books I gave you."

"Are we having a pop quiz tonight?"

He grinned. "Maybe."

"With a bonus like the one last night?"

He frowned. "About last night…"

"It was a mistake. I'm your employee. You're my boss."

"Exactly. It shouldn't have happened."

"You keep saying that, but then you keep kissing me."

"Only twice."

She grinned. "Third time's a charm."

"There won't be a third time. Come on, Lucky. Have a heart. I don't need this…you and me and this…thing between us. I've got responsibilities."

Her grin turned to full-blown smile. "We have a *thing* between us?"

"Damn, you're good."

"At what?"

He shook his head. "You're good, but I'm not falling for it, sweetheart. I can't. If you've got any smarts in that pretty head of yours, you'll leave well enough alone, stop trying to play me and concentrate on collecting your money."

"I'm playing you? How?"

He growled. "Study." Then he steered the horse around.

She watched him gallop away a few seconds later, her gaze straying from his broad shoulders to his tush sitting in the saddle, to the muscular thighs gripping the horse.

It wasn't a sight for the faint of heart, or the sexually deprived, and she had to literally force her gaze away.

Strangely enough, it wasn't the sight of him riding the horse that stayed in her mind. She kept picturing him by the break-fast table, that warm smile on his face as he stared down at his daughter.

The Texas heat, she told herself. She was getting punchy again, because who in their right mind would trade such a great image of buns for a scene out of "Father Knows Best"?

Not her, not with him. Tyler Grant wasn't viable husband material. But playing him... Now there was an intriguing thought.

With a smile on her face, Lucky started toward the house. She came to a jarring halt when she spotted Ulysses. He'd taken up residence in a rocker on the back porch. His cane sat across his knees, his hands gripping the chair arms.

Relax, she told herself. The man is as blind as Tyler is gorgeous. Just put one foot in front of the other and sneak by him. Easy. She took a deep breath and forced her legs to move, slowly, cautiously. She stepped onto the porch and headed for the doorway. Ulysses rocked back and forth a few feet to the right, mindless of her presence. She smiled. Piece of cake. Like taking candy from a baby—

Ulysses smacked his cane down to block her path. Lucky stumbled. "Got you!" he declared.

"Hey, what's the big idea?" Lucky grabbed at a porch post to regain her balance.

"Hush up and listen good." He pointed his cane at her. "I know your type, girlie, and don't you forget it."

"You know the unsophisticated, grease-monkey, Chicago-born-and-bred taxi-driver type?"

"Gold digger," Ulysses muttered. "Come runnin' out here to my ranch, flauntin' yourself to catch my boy and get your hands on his money, but I see right through them man-killer ways of yours, gal. A cab-driving nanny... Hah! A front, I tell you, and a damned poor one. But you mark my words, my boy sees right through you. He's known a lot of women like you, all tried to catch him, but not a one of 'em ever did. Married himself a gal with her own money. Lots of it." Ulys-ses poked her with his cane. "That's it, ain't it? That's what brought you out here, ain't it? Now he's got double the money, so's you're thinkin' to really cash in. Admit it, gal!''

Ulysses shoved the cane at her again, and Lucky barely resisted the urge to crack the blasted wood over his head. He was old and blind and obviously clueless. She was fairly sure God wouldn't let someone into heaven after she'd beat up on an old, helpless, blind man, no matter how provoking.

"Look, Mr. Grant. You're wrong. I'm not after Tyler's money. Well, okay, maybe a little of his money, but I'm earning that.''

"Yeah, I just bet you are.''

"I am. Oh no. I don't mean that kind of earning. I'm talking honest-to-goodness earn, as in work.''

"You think you can work yourself right into his wallet, reel him in like some bigmouth bass and he won't resist 'cause you know just how to ring his bells. Is that it, girlie? You huntin' my boy?''

"I'm not hunting anyone, especially your boy. I don't know the first thing about reeling in men or ringing their bells, though I was hoping to remedy that when I got back to Houston.''

"Sure you was, and I'm performin' brain surgery at noon today.'' He tapped his cane on the ground. "You mark my words. You let my boy alone and use those feminine wiles of yours on some other man.''

Wiles? She smiled. She had wiles?

"I'm watchin' you,'' Ulysses warned. "You ain't gettin' your hands on my boy or his money. He's stayin' right here where he belongs.'' He sat back in his chair. "Damn city slicker. A vamp, that's what you are. Well, you ain't vampin' my boy. Not no, but hell no…''

Ulysses's grumbling followed Lucky into the house and down the hallway. *A vamp*. She smiled wider. Vamp was good. Of course, sultry sexpot would have been better, but at least she'd moved up from flat-as-a-pancake Lucky.

She should have gone straight to her room the way Tyler had said. But the lure of the library and all those projector pieces distorted her rational thinking. All that machinery and nobody to put it back together.

Lucky went into the library and started sorting pieces. After fifteen minutes of careful scrutiny, she decided the thing was fixable. She begged a Phillips screwdriver, a flathead, and a wrench off of Mabel and went to work. Lucky was halfway into reconstructing the machine when a high-pitched scream shattered her concentration.

She bolted down the hall and followed Mabel and Bennie, who were already racing toward the living room. The three of them came to a staggering halt in the doorway, their gazes riveted on Helen, who sat in a mauve armchair, a cordless phone on her lap and a green lizard perched in her perfect silver coiffure.

"There's a *thing* on my head!" she shrieked, waving her arms excitedly. "Get it off! Get it off!"

Bennie dashed into the room and snatched the lizard from her grandmother's head.

"I—I was just sitting there on the phone and it just flew at me." Her frantic gaze went to Bernadette. "Don't panic, dear. Put it down slowly and Mabel can stomp it with her shoe—"

"Grandmother! That's murder!" Bennie stared down at the lizard. "And as for you, I've been worried sick about you."

"You...you..." Helen gasped and jumped to her feet, rubbing her arms as if a dozen creepy-crawlers swarmed over her. Her breaths came in short, ragged gasps. "You—you know this...this *lizard?*"

"Of course," Bennie said and shock gripped Helen's features. "And he didn't fly at you. Marlon doesn't fly, he crawls. He probably dropped from overhead."

"Marlon?"

"Yeah, he's my—"

"—nanny's pet," Lucky said, taking the lizard from Bennie. "Bad boy," she scolded. "Didn't Mommy Myers tell you to stay in your jar?'' *Mommy Myers?* Okay, so she didn't think fast on her feet. But hey, she was trying.

"So it's your lizard." A momentary flicker of relief passed Helen's features as she realized Lucky was the happy owner and not her granddaughter. Then the relief gave way to outrage and more harsh gasps. "My Bernadette's nanny is keeping a lizard!"

"Why, he's been in the family for years," Lucky exclaimed. "Used to belong to my granny, then my dad, and now me." Great. She was the proud owner of a hand-me-down lizard. "Are you all right? Marlon didn't hurt you, did he?"

"I think I'm…hyper…ventilating…need…to lie…down." Helen staggered toward the hallway. "Mabel, please…if you have a…paper bag."

"To put over your head?" Mabel beamed. "My pleasure, Helen. You just come with me."

"Sorry Marlon surprised you," Lucky called after Helen. "He just loves company."

"Thank you, thank you, thank you," Bennie said once she and Lucky were alone. "I owe you one."

"Ugh." Lucky handed the lizard over to Bennie. "How did he get out?"

"I sort of let him out."

"Why?"

"I hate the thought of him being cooped up in the terrarium. He deserves freedom like everyone else."

"Then let him loose in the backyard."

"So Jed's cat can have him? No way. Besides, Marlon's one of my best friends. Isn't that right, buddy?" Marlon blinked in answer and Bennie smiled. "Anyhow, I usually let him crawl around my room in the mornings. Marlon loves exercise." The exercise-lover in question curled up in Bennie's palm like a wet green noodle, his eyes closed.

"Yeah, I can see that," Lucky said. "He's a regular aerobics king."

"Thanks again." Bennie's gaze dropped to the lizard.

"Come on, Marlon. It's back to the torture chamber for us. Too bad you're not a math wizard instead of a lizard."

Chuckling, Bennie disappeared down the hallway and Lucky went back to the library. She scooped up the half-assembled projector and the rest of the parts and toted them back to her room. She could finish the job later, once she'd retrieved her toolbox from the trunk of the Chevy.

But now…

No more mothers-in-law, or flying lizards, or cranky old men wielding canes. Lucky was going to do what she should have done right after breakfast—hide in her room.

TWO HOURS LATER, Lucky stifled a yawn and willed her eyes open to the page in front of her. So much for reading to kill time. The words blurred and she slammed the book shut. She needed some fresh air or she'd wind up sleeping the day away—the longest Sunday of her entire life—and she couldn't, in good conscience, accept money for lazing around.

She was headed down the hall when she heard Bennie's voice.

"I *hate* this."

Lucky ducked her head into Bennie's room and saw the girl sitting at her desk wearing the dress Helen had brought her. "What's wrong?"

"Me," Bennie fumed. "I'm what's wrong. I'm not good at anything, least of all this stupid math. Mabel explained the percentage formula to me at least a dozen times this morning, but I still don't know what twenty percent of eighty-nine is and I don't care. I hate percentages, I hate math and I hate trying to do something I really hate, especially wearing this awful outfit. If I have to sit here a second longer, I'm liable to go blind." She rubbed her eyes, then covered her ears. "Or deaf. My head is just pounding and pounding and—"

"I know the feeling." Lucky walked into the room and stared at the textbook spread open on Bennie's cluttered desk.

A blur of math problems glared back at her. "Maybe you need a break."

She shook her head. "Daddy'll have my hide if I don't finish this stuff. Then there's the piano... Ugh, I hate Beethoven."

"Forget Beethoven for a little while. You need sunshine and fresh air. Your dad seems like a pretty humane guy. I'm sure he doesn't want you to go blind or deaf."

Bennie seemed to think about that for a long moment. "Well, fresh air does give you a new outlook sometimes. Besides, you're my nanny." She gave Lucky a smile. "I know Daddy wants me on my best and most cooperative behavior, and that means doing what I'm told, and that means taking a break if you say so."

"So where are we going?" Lucky asked once they were outside.

"To the barn. You like horses?"

"Mr. Ed was pretty cool."

"Mr. Who?"

"Never mind," Lucky said as Bennie dragged her toward the barn.

"This is Liz." Bennie introduced Lucky to a shiny brown horse with a white splotch on her face. "She's named after Elizabeth Taylor, Granddad's favorite actress."

"Your family's really into this old-movie stuff."

"Granddad loves movies, but Dad doesn't seem to like them much. Not the old ones, anyway, but he did take me to see *The Santa Clause* last year." She stroked the horse. "Liz is the best birthday present ever. Granddaddy gave her to me last month when I turned twelve."

"And you're already doing percentages? Isn't that illegal?"

"It should be." She fed Liz a sugar cube and pouted.

"Can I feed him?" Lucky took a sugar cube, held it out to the horse and said, "How many sugar cubes do you suppose an animal this large usually eats?"

"She can eat as many as ten."

"Let me see," Lucky glanced into the bucket and counted. "It looks like you've got about fifty percent of that. You might need to get some more."

Bennie frowned. "Oh no. I'm sure five is enough. I don't want to spoil her appetite for lunch."

"That's it," Lucky said with a smile.

"That's what?"

"You just told me what fifty percent of ten is. It's five."

"I did?" Bennie's eyes lit with excitement. "I did!"

"And it wasn't so bad. You didn't go blind or deaf or feel a second of pain."

"It was easy. I mean, fifty percent is half of something, and half of ten is five."

"What are you two doing?" Tyler's voice drew them both around to the barn door. Clothes streaked with dirt, he stood with a saddle balanced over one shoulder, work gloves on his hands and a frown on his face.

"I solved a percentage problem," Bennie declared.

"That's great, honey," he said, swiping at the sweat lining his forehead. "Why don't you run on inside and see what Mabel's got for lunch? I'm starved."

"You're not so bad, for a nanny," Bennie told Lucky before leaving the barn. She paused to give Tyler a smack on the cheek and an enthusiastic, "I did it!"

Tyler's gaze followed his daughter until she disappeared. Then he turned to Lucky.

She expected him to lay into her, to tell her how angry he was that she'd lured Bennie away from her studies. Instead, he smiled, that disarming smile that melted her defenses like hot popcorn melts butter.

"I've never seen her so excited over percentages before. Mabel isn't just my housekeeper and cook, she's a retired teacher who fills in as Bennie's tutor whenever we're between nannies. She's been trying to teach Bennie for weeks what you just did in a few minutes."

"Percentages are tough." Lucky grinned. "I ought to know,

I had the very same thing explained to me a long time ago, only it involved spark plugs and lug nuts.''

"You really love cars, don't you?''

"All kinds,'' she whispered. "But don't tell my Chevy. I wouldn't want her getting jealous.''

"What about me?'' The words came out so low, she almost didn't hear them. She wished she hadn't heard them. Then she wouldn't have to think about what they meant. Not that they really meant anything at all, she reminded herself. Tyler Grant didn't mean anything with all his teasing, his heated looks, his hungry gazes.

Wait a second. Hungry?

She did a double take, but the look in his eyes had faded. Deep, unreadable blue pools stared back at her.

Okay, forget hungry. Her imagination. Too much syrup on the pancakes this morning. Her brain was suffering from sugar rot. Nix the hunger idea and move on to something safe. "Why isn't Bennie going to school like every other kid?''

"Because Helen would come unglued if I put her in public school. She thinks Bennie is far above the average education system.''

"And what do you think?''

"I think she would do just fine in school with other kids her own age. *In*appropriate kids, as far as Helen's concerned.''

"You sure do pay a lot of attention to Helen's concerns.''

He shrugged. "I don't have a choice. She's my daughter's grandmother, and I don't want Bennie to ever feel caught in any disagreement between me and Helen. I want Bennie to have all the advantages. If she likes ranch life, fine. But if she ever has a craving for more, for Helen's world of ladyhood and tea parties and opera, I want her to feel comfortable with that, too. I want her to see all life has to offer and realize she can have everything. It isn't this life or that. She can fit in both worlds.''

"Like you?''

"Not like me.'' He shook his head. "I couldn't have it both

ways, but Bennie can. She will.'' He lifted the edge of his shirt and wiped at his sweaty forehead again. When he finally spoke, his voice was considerably softer. "You're doing a good job with her. I really appreciate it."

"Good, because I've got a proposition for you." She faced him. "I'm supposed to be Bennie's temporary nanny, so why don't I actually *be* the nanny?" When he looked doubtful, she rushed on, "I can't stand sitting around doing nothing and getting paid for it. I want to earn the money you're forking over. I'm not prep-school polished, but I'm educated enough to be a darn good tutor. Besides, Helen is sure to be suspicious if she sees Mabel tutoring Bennie. That's the nanny's job."

"All right," he said after weighing the idea for a few seconds. "You can help with her schoolwork and oversee her piano and French lessons, but I still want you to stay as far away from Helen as possible."

"No problem. Consider me invisible." Which wasn't so far from the truth, at least for her chest. "I'm going to earn every penny of that money, you'll see."

"Oh, I plan on seeing, all right. Two weeks is a long time. You'll only be able to hide from Helen for so long before she gets ahold of you. Then it'll be showtime."

"Meaning?"

"We're still on for our nightly lessons. You're fine in the academic department, but we need to work on your social skills." He shrugged. "And since we'll be working so closely together, we need to get something straight."

"No kissing."

"No kissing, no questions about kissing, or any other related topic. Strictly business."

"Whatever you say, boss. But you're the one who keeps kissing me."

"Don't remind me."

"Speaking of which, if you want a business relationship, why do you keep doing that—"

"Cut it out. I'm serious. No more questions. And don't look at me like that."

"Like what?"

"Like that." He gestured toward her. "With your eyes so wide, your lips parted like that and that expression."

"What expression—"

He growled and spun on his heel, and though Lucky had no firsthand experience, she had the inexplicable feeling that she'd just seen her first sexually frustrated man. And that she'd been the responsible party.

About time!

LUCKY SPENT the next several evenings with Tyler, and though she broached the subject of their kisses many times, he never failed to cut her off, and he was careful to keep his distance. Drat the man. How was she supposed to get this man-woman stuff down if he insisted on being so stubborn? And grouchy?

"You could smile once in a while. Your face won't break," she told him Wednesday.

"Remember all this stuff I'm teaching you and I'll smile."

"You drive a hard bargain." Lucky fidgeted in her chair.

"Just concentrate. You don't have to memorize every word. I just want you to have a general view of Helen's world and what she expects. Now, everyone who's anyone lives in River Oaks."

"I know the area like the back of my hand." Lucky launched into a description of streets and landmarks and Tyler frowned.

"Forget potholes and stop signs. You need to be familiar with some of the prominent families, such as…"

The list of Houston's elite seemed endless, but Lucky memorized every name, trivia about the families, Helen's charity contacts, and of course, Smithston. Not that Tyler had to tell Lucky anything about the elite school. It was all Helen talked about at dinner every night.

"Smithston is simply divine," Helen declared over pot roast

on Thursday. "All three of Louise's daughters graduated from Smithston, and all of them married very well, I might add."

"That wouldn't be Louise Cromwell, would it?" Lucky stared across the table at Helen, watching her eyes widen in surprise. It was now or never. Either she shared some of her new knowledge or her brain was bound to explode from overload.

"Why, yes, it would. Don't tell me you know Louise?"

"Not personally, mind you. But she did a wonderful job with that fund-raiser for the Houston Ballet last season." Lucky smiled and Helen frowned.

"But I thought you were in Scotland last season?"

So much for showing off. "Well, uh, yes, but good news travels fast, and it was such a worthy cause."

Helen stared at Lucky for a long moment, those dark eyes assessing. Finally she smiled. In the nick of time, too. Lucky could feel the sweat beads about to pop out on her forehead.

"Louise is a genius, and one of my dearest friends. Perhaps she could help me with all this trouble I'm having with the museum fund-raiser. I simply have to find a new location. I've been on the phone every day, all day, and each place I call is already booked."

"Guthrie's Barbecue. They do fund-raisers," Ulysses declared. "Hosted the Texas Cattlemen Association's annual cook-off last year. Got the best ribs this side of the Rio Grande."

"Barbecue? Really, Ulysses. I need a ballroom, a concert hall, something appropriate for the affair."

"Affair, my behind."

"Now that is uncalled for," Helen huffed. "Do you have to be so vulgar every time you open your mouth?"

"No, I can eat, too. But it's more fun ribbin' you. You know, you got a vein the size of Texas that pokes out on your forehead when you're mad—"

"Dad!" Tyler cut in.

"Uh, not that I can see it, mind you." Ulysses groped for

his water glass, his swollen red eyes fixed on the air in front of him. "My old sight still hasn't come back. But I remember clear as day how it did look."

"Rude," Helen said scornfully. "That's what you are."

"Snooty. That's what you are."

"Buzzard."

"Old fuddy-duddy."

And the insults went on and on with Tyler playing referee, Bennie smiling and Lucky doing her best not to laugh. As stressful as this nanny business was, it was the most fun Lucky had had in a long time, which spoke volumes for her lousy social life. But no more. In just over a week she returned home, richer and wiser, and she was going to nab the first available good-looking man she found.

Hurry! Hurry! her hormones chanted. If only her heart were half as enthusiastic.

WHILE LUCKY'S NIGHTS were filled with facts and headaches, her days were spent with Bernadette. Helen, thank goodness, was preoccupied with getting her gala back on track. The moment her plans fell into place, something happened to upset them and she was back on the phone. First, it was the location. Then she spent hours looking for a florist. Then the band cancelled. She stayed so busy she spared Lucky only a few harried glances. Thanks to Tyler.

He'd told Lucky he was a well-connected investment banker, a very successful one, but that image of him never quite fit with the rugged cowboy she saw day after day. As much trouble as Helen was having, however, Lucky had no doubt that Tyler had friends in very high places.

Helen's preoccupation gave Lucky and Bernadette some time to themselves, to study and do other things Lucky deemed were ladylike endeavors.

"I don't see why we have to do this," Bennie said one day. "I hate high heels and you hate high heels and I'm never going to wear them and you shouldn't, either, otherwise you'll wind up with bunions and calluses and all kinds of gross stuff like that.''

"We're not learning this because we have to, Bennie. We're doing it because we want to. For your dad. All this is really important to him.''

Bennie gave a heavy sigh and nodded. "Oh, all right. For Daddy.'' She balanced the book on her head, stepped into the inch-high shoes and wobbled across the room. She also started wearing a dress every evening to dinner, and putting in extra time at the piano. Score one for Lucky the nanny.

Now, if Lucky the woman had been half as successful. Tyler—damn his stubborn, professional hide—had gone from flirty and fun to stuffy and preoccupied, and Lucky was back to fantasizing about Buster and push-up bras.

"STELLA, how's my granny?'' Lucky asked Friday evening when she phoned the cab company.

"Fine—''

"It's been a full week and I'm going crazy without you,'' Buster declared, ripping the phone from Stella's hand.

"Really?'' She smiled. "You miss me?''

"Hell, yes! The Kangaroos creamed us. Stella's game stinks worse than Georgie Petrie's bowling shoes.''

"Stella?''

"She filled in for you. We had to have another person or the league would've disqualified us. When are you coming back? Because I lost a load of money, not to mention there's this new girl at the shoe counter that I want to impress, and losing isn't exactly impressive...''

"You missed my *bowling?*'' Her smile dissolved and she had the sudden vision of herself bowling a perfect strike with Buster's face as the tenth pin. "Rest assured, I'll be back soon,'' she vowed with tight lips. "How's my granny?''

"Fine. I ain't had my visit yet, my turn's tomorrow, but between all of us, somebody's looked in on her every day.''

"Tell everybody thanks for me.''

"Talk is cheap. If you're really thankful, get your carcass back here. We play the Munson Cab Magpies tomorrow night and…"

Buster went on about the new shoe girl and the whopping fifty bucks he had riding on the next game.

Forget Buster, she told herself once she managed to hang up a few minutes later. Who cared if he missed her? She didn't.

And she certainly didn't care one way or another if Tyler Grant kissed her again, the jerk. She would just get some practice somewhere else. Tyler wasn't the only man in the world.

At least that's what her hormones—those vocal devils—kept saying. If only the rest of her could agree.

9

"LUCKY, I'm in deep trouble!" Bernadette stood in the doorway of Lucky's bedroom Saturday morning. "Grandmother saw Marlon in my room. I told her I was baby-sitting him for you and I think she bought it, but anyway, she got this funny look in her eyes. I think she wants to take him back to Houston and have him made into shoes!"

"He's a three-inch lizard." Lucky put aside her screwdriver and stared at the antique projector, fully intact and operational once again. "What's she going to make? Barbie shoes?"

"Please," Bernadette pleaded. "He needs a new mommy."

At the distraught look on her face, Lucky nodded and found herself quickly cradling the limp lizard. "I'm not really the nurturing type. I've got a houseful of dead plants, small children cry and hit me with candy and... Oh Geez, I think he's really dead this time." Yuck. She was holding a dead lizard. Okay, so dead might be good in this case. A quick flush down the toilet and her mommy days would be over.

"He's just tired." Bernadette peered at Marlon, then poked him with a finger. "He sleeps a lot."

"I don't know," she said, then Marlon promptly blinked, killing the toilet fantasy. "Okay, so he's not dead, but I still don't know about this mommy business—"

"Bernadette! I'm choosing flowers for the centerpieces and I would like your opinion."

"Quick," Bennie said, yanking Lucky to her feet. "Get out of here and take Marlon to safety."

"Don't you think you're overreacting?"

"Grandmother loves to wear dead animals. She has an entire closetful of them. I won't let her add Marlon to the list."

"Okay." Lucky let Bennie pull her out the door and shove her down the hallway. "But you owe me, big time."

"Anything you want."

"Tea lessons. All refined ladies drink tea. I found a great book about it in your dad's library, complete with a video demonstrating appropriate tea behavior."

Helen's footsteps sounded closer and Bennie nodded frantically. "Anything, just take a hike for a little while and if Grandmother asks, you never even saw Marlon."

"Don't I wish," Lucky said once Bennie had disappeared. "But I guess we're stuck with each other." She slid Marlon into her pocket and headed out to the barn to kill some time.

"Dadblasted hired hands. If you want something done right, you got to do it yourself."

She turned to see Ulysses standing in an empty horse stall, a shovel in one hand.

Uh-oh. She started to back out, but Ulysses turned his angry red eyes in her direction.

"Hold it right there, girlie. You spyin' on me?"

"Uh, no. I was just taking a walk."

"Likely story." He turned back to shovel a pile of manure. "Well, hell's bells," he grumbled over his shoulder. "Stop spyin' and come on over here and give me a hand. This barn needs to be cleaned out from top to bottom."

"Should you be doing all of this in your condition?"

"I'm as fit as a fiddle, missy."

"But your eyes…"

"I worked this ranch my entire life and I'll be damned if I'm going to stop now. Jed and Tyler are overworked as it is. Hands are scarce. Here—" he motioned her toward a water hose "—make yours useful. That concrete aisle needs hosing."

"But—"

"Ain't afraid of a little work, are you, city gal?"

"Work, no. Lunatic old men with shovels, yes."

He glared at her for a long, silent moment, and Lucky barely resisted the urge to turn and run. She should. He had a shovel and he hated her. He could bop her on the head and bury her and no one would be the wiser.

Except maybe Bennie. Yeah, the little girl was sure to miss Marlon who'd be six feet under since he was tucked away in Lucky's pocket. She stiffened and held Ulysses's stare. Just let the old guy try to bop her. She'd shatter his precious projector all over again. Then he could put it back together himself.

After what seemed like eternity, he chuckled. Okay, so maybe the old geezer wasn't so bad and, of course, she could never destroy something she'd put hours into restoring.

He directed Lucky to hose down the concrete walkway that ran between the stalls, then set about shoveling more manure from the dirt floor of the stall. They worked for the next fifteen minutes in companionable silence and Lucky actually started to enjoy herself. Other than the smell—*and what smell!*—she rather liked having something to do besides the lady lessons she'd been torturing Bennie and herself with. She sprayed her way toward the end of the aisle, then turned to work her way back up.

"What's going on in here?"

Her head jerked up and she saw the unmistakable shadow of Tyler Grant in the barn doorway. She heard Ulysses's shovel hit the dirt a second before he walked out of the stall and straight into her line of fire. The spray hit him full force and he stumbled backward.

She let go of the handle and the water dwindled. "Oh, Geez, are you all right—"

"Help, boy, she's killing me!"

What?

Tyler sent her a murderous look, rushed to Ulysses's side and helped the man who stumbled and groped along the aisle as if he couldn't see two inches in front of his face. "Dad, what the devil is going on?"

"I heard a ruckus and I come out here to find this city gal makin' a mess out of my barn. I tried to stop her, son, but you saw what happened. Little filly's got a temper and I couldn't get within two feet of her."

He was lying. The man was lying, and Tyler believed him!

"Never ever wander out of the house again without somebody with you, Dad." Tyler helped Ulysses toward the barn door.

"What's all the ruckus?" Mabel met them just inside the doorway. "Ulysses? Are you all right?"

"Thanks to my boy here. You saved me, son. I don't know what an old man like me would do without you." Ulysses put on his most pathetic pout for Mabel. "Honey, my backside aches something fierce and I sure am hungry."

Tyler handed Ulysses over to Mabel and turned on Lucky, a frown carving his face.

"You didn't believe that, did you?" she demanded. "Why, I never heard a bigger bunch of…" Her words dwindled when Ulysses motioned frantically to her from just behind Tyler, and suddenly the situation became crystal clear. An act. A poor helpless act, and a pretty pitiful one. And Tyler believed it.

"Go on," Tyler growled at Lucky. "You were saying?"

"I never heard a bigger… Oh, all right. You caught me." *Sucker,* her conscience chided. Okay, so she was. A lizard-sitting sucker who had a heart.

Ulysses smiled and disappeared with Mabel, leaving Lucky to face Tyler on her own. Showdown at the OK Corral.

"Are you crazy?" he bellowed. "You could have killed my dad with that damned water hose! I know you don't like him, but—"

"Listen, buddy." She planted her hands on her hips. Suckers had their limits like everybody else. "It was an accident. Here I was trying to help out and he walked into my line of fire.'' She gripped the handle and aimed the hose at him. "Just like you're doing right now.''

"You wouldn't dare.''

"Oh, wouldn't I?''

"Dammit to hell!'' he sputtered, arms raised to ward off the sudden spray of water.

Lucky soaked him good from head to boots before her courage faded and her lust took over. The hose went limp in her hands.

Water slid down Tyler's tanned face, the strong column of his throat. His drenched T-shirt molded to the hard muscles of his torso. Geez, he looked good wet. Too good. Too mad. He shoved dripping hair from his face and stalked toward her.

He reached her in three strides, gripped her upper arms and Lucky clamped her eyes shut. She couldn't stand the sight of blood, especially her own, and Tyler had murder on his mind.

He kissed her full on the mouth.

His lips were hard, insistent, not that they had to be. She softened immediately, her lips parting for the searching heat of his tongue. He devoured her for one fast and furious moment before he broke the contact to stare down at her, an unreadable expression in his eyes.

"I'm crazy,'' he muttered. Then he released her and stalked out of the barn, leaving Lucky dazed and confused and on fire.

She took a deep breath, turned the hose on herself and let the water fly.

OF ALL THE CABDRIVERS in Houston, Tyler had to wind up with Lucky. And she thought she was the unlucky one?

His tomboyish ugly duckling had turned into a swan. An intelligent, compassionate swan who got along with his daughter, which wasn't the problem in itself.

He was the problem. The way his heart did that funny double thump when she smiled at him, and the way he caught himself smiling back when he'd already decided not to, the way he leaned closer when she passed by him, the way his palms itched to reach out, to touch her. Hell, the way he had touched her, kissed her.

It was her fault. She was an expert at seducing men. She had to be or he wouldn't be falling so hard, so damned fast.

Or *getting* hard so damned fast, he thought later that evening when Lucky met him in the library for their lesson. Just the sight of her in cutoff blue-jean shorts and a white T-shirt pumped his blood faster. He tore his gaze from her and concentrated on uncorking two wine bottles.

"What's this?" She plopped down in the chair while he perched on the edge of the desk. "I thought you just wanted me to have a general knowledge of wines, in case the subject came up. I didn't know there was going to be an actual quiz."

"One week down, but we've still got a full seven days to go. I thought if you wowed Helen by choosing a bottle of wine, it would win you a few brownie points. Now," he said, indicating one of the bottles, "this is a white chardonnay."

"Chicken or seafood," she said with a pleased smile.

"Not bad, but we need details." He poured the pale liquid into a glass and held it up to the lamp for a quick study. "Light in color, almost like a sauvignon blanc." He held the rim to his nose. "Green apples and vanilla." He took a sip and savored the subtle burst of flavor. "Soft and fragrant..." He smiled at her. "Overall, a very well-balanced wine." He poured her a glass. "Your turn."

She took a tentative sip and went through the spiel.

"Good. Now, this chardonnay will be served with the salad and soup. After that," he said, reaching for the next bottle, "It's on to the main course and this 1991 Beringer Private Reserve cabernet sauvignon." He recited more tasting notes then handed her a glass. "Try it."

Taking a deep breath, she sipped the wine. She didn't miss a word or a gesture, the recitation ending on a huge hiccup. "Oops, sorry." Another hiccup. "I guess my system's not really used to this. I'll try not to do that tomorrow night."

She smiled, and for once the library's paneled walls didn't

seem so gloomy, or the old movie paraphernalia a painful reminder. Not with Lucky across from him.

She sat cross-legged in her chair, her bare feet curled beneath her, her face free and clear of makeup, her hair pulled back in a simple hairband. Her eyes were warm chocolate, her cheeks glowing from the wine she'd consumed, and Tyler knew he'd never seen a woman look more beautiful.

She hiccuped again and took another drink. "This isn't bad."

"It shouldn't be at sixty dollars a bottle."

She choked on her next mouthful. "Sixty dollars?"

"Don't look so shocked. A first-growth Château Margeaux or Château Latour Bordeaux can go for two hundred dollars."

"It is good," she admitted, taking another sip. She stared at him for a long moment. "You know, I'm trying really hard to picture you in an expensive suit, forking over two hundred dollars for a bottle of wine, but I can't. You seem more like the beer-drinking, hell-raising type."

"I am. I just tried to pretend for a while that I wasn't."

"Well, if it's any consolation, I like the hell-raising type, though I don't know much about the beer part. I've never tried beer." She sipped her wine, hiccuped and smiled. "But this stuff is pretty good."

It was all he could do to keep from leaning forward and tasting her wine-wet lips. Just a leisurely trail of his tongue across her full bottom lip... Today, he'd been too worked up to take it slow. And he wanted it slow.

Hell, he wanted it fast, too.

Slow, fast, any way he could get it with her. *Her.* The realization hit him like a lightning bolt straight to his groin. As if that wasn't enough to fry his control, she decided to make matters worse.

"Why don't you kiss me?" Before he could answer, she stood and leaned into him. "Never mind. I'll kiss you." Her lips were soft and warm and full.

"Why did you do that?" he asked when she pulled away.

"I've been wanting to kiss you all day since the barn, then you didn't kiss me, so I kissed you and—"

"I meant stop. Why did you stop?" Before she could answer, he captured her lips again. She tasted of wine and woman and desire and he couldn't help himself. He moved her around, tipped her back over the desk and followed her down. He pressed into the cradle of her thighs. His tongue tangled with hers in a long breathless kiss that ended on a hiccup.

"Sorry," she breathed, "but you're making my head spin."

He grinned. "That's the wine."

"No," she said in all seriousness. "It's you." And the way she stared at him with all that wide-eyed innocence while her fingers traced naughty circles over the bulge in his jeans, it was all he could do not to embarrass himself.

"Ah, that feels so good," she said, her eyes closed, her lips curved into a smile.

"You feel good." He trailed a fingertip along her cheek, then dipped his head to follow the path with soft kisses. "You taste good, too."

"You've got great hands, Tyler." She wiggled underneath him. "Stop that," she said hoarsely. "No, don't stop. I love it."

Him kissing her cheek? She'd go crazy with a little ear nibbling. He leaned down and ran the tip of his tongue along the delicate shell.

She moaned, "Ahhhhhhhh," and caught her bottom lip, her eyes closed, her body arching. "Oooooooooo."

He dipped his tongue into her ear and she came off the desk.

"I can't take it. Stop... Don't stop... I can't breathe." She gasped and he pulled away to stare at her face. "I said not to stop," she said, her eyes still closed, her lips curving. "That tickles. Oh, ah, not there..." She giggled and squirmed. "Keep going. Yeah, touch me just like that. Right there..."

"Lucky, I'm not touching you."

"Of course you are. I can feel you. Ooooooo, yes. Yes!"

"I'm not touching you!"

Her eyes snapped open and her smile faded. He leaned away from her and they both stared down the length separating them.

"Ah-ha! There you are, you bad boy!" She sat up and scooped Marlon off the inside of her thigh. "Mommy Myers was worried about you." She glanced up at Tyler. "I, uh, this is my recent adoptee."

"It's Bennie's lizard."

"She gave him to me. She's afraid Helen will make shoes out of him."

"I feel like making shoes out of him." He glared at Marlon before letting out a deep breath. "I'm insane. I'm envious of a damned lizard."

"Lizard envy," she said. "Is that anything like—"

"Close." He kissed her again, long and hard and desperate. "He got to third base and I'm still stuck in the batting cage."

"But you're up to bat now." She sat Marlon on a nearby chair and faced Tyler. "And if you swing as good as Marlon," she grinned, "I'd say you'll make it to third base."

"What about a home run?"

A dream, Lucky thought the moment the words sang through her head. This had to be a dream because no way in her ordinary, boring life would a tall, dark and dangerous cowboy be telling her he wanted to...

"I want you, Lucky. Now."

Way. She swallowed and tried to keep her heart from jumping right out of her chest. "This isn't like the last time, where you kiss me then change your mind—"

He touched two fingertips to her lips. "Now," he whispered again, kissing her hungrily. He swept her into his arms and strode through the darkened house. When they reached his bedroom, he slid her to her feet.

"We can't, not with everyone just down the hall—"

Another kiss silenced her. "I just need to get something." He disappeared inside while she shifted nervously in the hallway and did her best to keep from shouting hallelujah! It was really going to happen. Him and her. Together!

He came up behind her, a blanket in one arm, his shirt pocket stuffed full of foil packets. Condoms.

"Are we going to use all of those?"

He grinned. "We're going to give it one hell of a shot. Come on." He grabbed her hand and they headed outside. Behind the barn, they mounted a staircase that led to the second floor and a single doorway. Tyler paused to kiss her before he unlocked the door and led Lucky inside.

"What is this place?"

"The ranch foreman's office." He tossed the blanket on a nearby desk, slammed and locked the door behind them, then turned to the sofa. In seconds he'd folded it out into a bed that took up nearly the entire room.

"What if he comes back?"

He reached for her. "I'm the ranch foreman."

"Oh." She smiled up at him and his mouth touched hers.

Tyler's kiss was better this time, deeper, hungrier, more urgent, and much more frightening. But the urgency and fear were nothing compared to the desperate heat swirling through her body. Her nipples throbbed, her legs quivered, her insides ached.

Before she knew what was happening, he lifted her onto the desk, swept a stack of ledgers, a coffee mug and several pictures onto the floor, then pressed her onto her back. Large, strong hands worked at the buttons of her fly. He swept denim and panties off in one smooth motion, then parted her legs. Settling himself between them, he pulled her full against him.

She felt his hard length beneath his jeans. He rubbed against her, rough denim brushing sensitive flesh, and the friction made her gasp. He caught the sound with his mouth. His tongue tangled with hers to coax small, eager whimpers from her throat. He nibbled a path down her jaw, the slope of her neck.

She glanced down just in time to see him push up her T-shirt and free her breasts. A lifetime of insecurity kicked in and she struggled to cover herself. She didn't want to ruin things this time with an attack of the invisible, flat-chested woman.

"Don't," she said, shoving the shirt down.

He pushed the fabric back up and stared while Lucky's heart literally stopped beating. "I wonder," he murmured after an endless moment, "if they taste as good as they look."

Before she could even think of a reply, he dipped his head, drew one swollen nipple into his mouth, and shot Lucky's notions about men and chest preferences clear to the moon.

"Do they?" she asked breathlessly when he pulled away to scorch a path up the curve of her neck to her pulse beat.

"Do they what?"

"Taste as good?"

He lifted his head and smiled down at her, that all-too-familiar naked-stranger smile that made her nerves tingle. "Better," he said. "But I'm not through tasting." His weight shifted and his body slid lower. Then his mouth touched the inside of one bare thigh. "Eat your heart out, Marlon."

Tyler loved her with his mouth, his tongue, touching and tasting and heating her body. Then she exploded, crying out his name as a sweet river of sensation flooded over her, through her.

"I want to taste every inch of you." He trailed his fingers over the moist heat between her legs. "Feel you." His voice was ragged. "I'm damn near ready to burst just thinking about it."

"Then stop thinking and start doing."

"Impatient," he murmured. "I like that."

"Desperate," she said, "and I don't like it. *Do* something."

He grinned and caught her mouth in a hungry kiss. Then he scooped her into his arms and eased her down onto the mattress. He pulled the T-shirt over her head then stood back to unbutton his shirt. It slid away from his chest, down his arms and hit the floor. His boots followed. A zipper hissed and his jeans and briefs joined the pile of clothing.

She'd never seen a man naked before. Okay, well, she'd seen *Tyler* naked before—in the river. But no one else. Not in person, and, well, movies didn't come close to this. To *him*. Dark hair sprinkled his chest, swirling to an enticing line that headed for his navel, then lower…

She swallowed. He grinned. Then he grabbed a foil packet, slid on a condom and lowered his body to hers.

Panic swamped her all of five seconds as the tip of his hardness probed her throbbing heat. He brushed soft kisses on her lips, her eyelids, murmured explicit words of exactly what he wanted to do to her, and her initial fear passed.

"Oh, Lucky, you're so tight," he whispered a moment before he braced himself and plunged into her. "Oh no. Oh *no*. A *virgin?*" He stilled his movements, but it was too late.

Pain splintered through her and she clamped her eyes shut. "Just—just a formality," she mumbled as a scalding tear squeezed past her lashes to burn down her cheek.

"You're crying." He caught the drop with his tongue.

"I am not," she whispered back after a few heartbeats, "I— I never cry. Ever." Thankfully the tears dissolved as quickly as the pain. She moved her hips and relished the rush of sensation that shimmied through her.

"If you don't stop that, you'll make me lose control."

"Good. I don't want you in control. I want you totally out of control, and completely inside me." She lifted her pelvis, drew him deeper and he let out a low moan.

"Demanding," he said as he started to move inside her. His face eased into a grin. "I like that, too."

Then there were no more words, only a flood of sensation as he drove into her, slow at first, then faster, deeper, until she couldn't take any more.

She cried out. Her body burst into a thousand colorful specks while her hormones finally let loose that hallelujah victory cry and joined Tyler's fierce groan as he followed her into the land of the sexually satisfied.

Seconds later, he leaned away from her. "What did you say? It sounded like hal—"

"Nothing." She shook her head. *Everything*. She'd done it. And with him. And it had been great—

"I'm a jerk."

"You," she declared, "were wonderful."

"And you," he said, leaning up on one elbow to stare down at her, "were a virgin. Hell, I never even thought…"

"I didn't exactly have 'virgin' tattooed on my forehead."

"No, but the way you looked, all that wide-eyed innocence. I thought it was an act, that you were used to seducing men."

"Me?" She smiled and pushed him onto his back to straddle him. "A seductress? Really?" He nodded and her smile widened, then her gaze shot to the pile of condoms. "One down and a few dozen to go."

"Damn, woman. A guy can only do so much."

She shrugged and pretended indifference. "Well, if you can't keep up…keep *it* up…" She started to move away, but an iron hand gripped her arm.

"*It* doesn't want you to go. I think you've made a new best friend."

"Just how friendly can I be?" She touched him gently, and grinned at his indrawn breath. "What about something a little…friendlier?" She mounted him, sliding down his length until he was full and throbbing inside her. "How about that?"

He nodded, his face severe, the muscles in his neck bulging. "Yeah, friendly's good." He gritted his teeth.

"Just good?" She moved, and flames licked at her senses.

"Great," he growled. "Greater than great." His hands cupped her buttocks and rocked her in a slow, gentle motion.

Then she lost herself in the wonderful feeling of loving Tyler Grant.

THE SLAM OF A DOOR jerked Lucky awake. "Tyler, wake up," she whispered. A heavy footfall on the steps below punctuated her words. "Tyler, come on. There's someone downstairs!"

His eyes snapped open. "Dammit," he breathed, his gaze darting to the windows where sunlight blazed just outside. Then he was on his feet, pulling on his jeans.

"I overslept." He worked at his zipper. "It's morning," he growled. *"Morning."*

"I knew we shouldn't have done this with so many people nearby." Lucky wrung her hands as the footsteps moved closer, climbing the stairs outside. Her gaze riveted on the door. "What are we going to do? Everybody will know. Helen will know," she said in a rush of words. "And your father, and he warned me not to ring your bells and now he'll think I'm loose and easy, the wicked city girl come to claim his baby boy—"

"Shh." He peered past the drapes.

"Easy for you to say. You men have it so easy. You get a pat on the back while we women…"

We women. The words struck her like a lightning bolt from the femininity gods. A woman. A fully initiated, red-blooded, sexually active goddess extraordinaire!

"It's just Jed," Tyler told her. "He's probably looking for me. We've got a huge cattle shipment coming in today and I should have been up hours ago." He shrugged on his shirt and grabbed his boots. "I'll head him off at the pass. Wait ten minutes, then get dressed and go back to the house. And remember everything we went over about the wine. You're going solo with Helen tonight. I've already lost several hours of work. There's no way I'll make it back in time for dinner. Lucky?" He frowned. "Did you hear me?"

She nodded. "Wine, Helen." A woman. A real woman.

"And behave yourself." His gaze narrowed. "Are you okay?"

"Never better," she mumbled, waving him off just as Jed reached the top step outside.

Tyler stared at her, his face serious, contemplating for the space of two heartbeats. He strode over to give her a quick, hungry kiss. Then he was gone, the door closing behind him.

Once the voices outside faded, she crawled out of bed and floated into the small office bathroom. Her body tingled, her insides ached.

A woman!

She looked the same, she thought as she gazed into the mirror, yet she didn't. There was something about her eyes— a knowing that lit up the dark depths. And her mouth—pink and swollen from a night of passionate kisses. And her cheeks—full and rosy. She looked...like a woman.

"Eat your heart out, Marlon. You've been replaced."

10

OKAY, so maybe Lucky had fibbed when she'd promised to behave. But everybody knew you didn't let a car sit for days on end without letting the engine run a few minutes, and it had been so long since she'd been behind the wheel of her cab. Besides, with Helen still busy trying to line up a new band for her gala—the first *three* had miraculously cancelled—and Bernadette tasting practice pies for Mabel's entry in the annual Hickory pie competition, the coast was clear. And Lucky needed something, anything, to keep her mind off last night.

She still couldn't believe it. She'd floated through most of the morning, happy and dazed. Then she'd encountered Tyler out by the barn, getting ready to ride out, and reality had set in. She'd given him a brilliant smile and he'd barely tipped his hat. His face had been a stoic mask, his eyes shuttered with regret. A mistake, his look told her. We made a mistake.

So maybe they had in terms of their situation, but Lucky refused to let that fact color her happiness. This was her moment of triumph. Victory. She'd lost her virginity and she'd loved every moment. She refused to feel ashamed or regretful for something so wonderful, so…right, whether he wanted to admit it or not.

She forced Tyler from her thoughts and climbed into her cab. The engine purred to life. Ahhh. Her Chevy she could count on. Men would come and go, but this car would always be there. No matter what she looked like, how small her breasts, how long her legs. The engine missed, sputtered, and her happiness dissolved.

"*Et tu, Brute?*"

She had the sleeves of her navy silk blouse rolled up, her toolbox out of the trunk and the hood popped in that next instant. Relief swept through her. Just a bad plug.

"Hey there, Miss Lucky."

"Billy?" Panic swept through her as she stared at the pudgy officer outlined in the open garage door. "What are you doing here?"

"Me and Hank came out to talk to Tyler, but he ain't here."

"Um, Billy, you didn't happen to see Tyler's mother-in-law, did you?" The last thing she needed was Billy and Hank blowing her cover.

"Cain't say that I had that pleasure. Mabel said she was taking a nap, something about a headache over some fund-raiser."

Thank heavens, Lucky thought.

"Hank's in the kitchen saying hello to Ulysses," Billy went on. "But he'll be along any minute. Haven't seen much of Ulysses since his surgery. We miss him at bingo. Nice old guy—"

"Billy!" Hank came barreling around the side of the house. "What the hell did you do to the patrol car?"

"I turned it off."

"Well, the engine won't start."

"Hi, Mr. Hank," Lucky said.

He spared her a quick glance and said, "Howdy, little lady," then did a fast double take. "*You're* the city gal Ulysses was talking about?"

"Yep," Billy chimed in. "She's Tyler's temporary nanny."

"How temporary?" Hank asked.

"Two weeks. One down. One to go."

"Good," he grumbled, turning toward Billy. "The blasted battery's dead or somethin'."

"Does it make any sound?" Lucky asked.

"Not a peep," Hank replied, his comment directed at Billy.

"Then it's probably not the battery," Lucky said. "Unless it's old."

"Battery's brand new," he said over his shoulder.

"What about the connectors?"

"They're fine, too. Now, Billy, I want you to go call Jess and tell him I need him out here—"

"Are you sure?" Lucky cut in. "Because if the engine's not turning over, it's obviously not getting any juice. And if the battery's new, then it has to be the connectors."

Hank glared. "And what do you know about connectors?"

Lucky rubbed her hands together. "Can I take a look?"

Billy nodded, Hank grumbled, and Lucky grabbed her tool-box and headed for the patrol car sitting out front. She popped the hood, took one look at the battery and smiled. "It's your connectors, all right. They're corroded. You have to keep them clean. If you don't get a good solid connection to your battery, it can be dangerous." She spent the next half hour cleaning and replacing the connectors. The engine purred to life.

"Thanks," Hank muttered grudgingly, shoving his hand out for a shake.

Lucky accepted the gesture, knowing it was probably harder for him than passing a kidney stone. "Any time."

"When is Tyler going to be back?" Hank asked, once he and Billy had climbed into the car.

"Late tonight."

"I already told Ulysses, but he was busy eating some of Mabel's pie and I don't know if he heard everything. We've got pictures being faxed to us from an airport in New York. Seems that thieving city woman tried to sell Tyler's watch. A surveillance camera got her on tape. We need Tyler to identify her. Tell him to drive into town as soon as he can."

"Did they catch her?"

"Dadblamed woman got away, but the police up there have a few leads. She purchased a plane ticket for Canada. They radioed the authorities there, and she'll have quite a surprise waiting for her, if it is her. That's what we need Tyler for. Ulysses never got a good look at her, what with his eyes and all, and Mabel says she thinks she can identify her, but she'd hate to be wrong, so that leaves Tyler.''

"I'll be sure to tell him."

"Thanks again, Miss Lucky," Billy said.

"Yeah," Hank agreed, and Lucky couldn't help but smile.

An expression that dissolved the minute she turned and saw Helen standing in the library's huge bay window, watching her.

She swallowed the sudden lump in her throat and waved.

Not that it did any good, she realized when she noted the grease covering her hands, the open toolbox at her feet.

As she packed up her tools, she contemplated climbing into her cab and making a run for it. Tyler was going to be mad as hell if Helen told him.

If Helen had even seen anything. Maybe she'd just glanced out the window at that moment. Maybe she was nearsighted and had glimpsed nothing more than a few blobs of color. Maybe lightning would strike Lucky and she'd be spared having to explain anything to Tyler once he returned.

But then, Lucky Myers had never been very lucky.

Night fell crisp and clear, no lightning bolts in sight. Not even a little thunder. Helen, as it turned out, had twenty-twenty eyesight, and had seen the entire car-fixing episode. Lucky's ad-lib about the Scottish chauffeur showing her a bit of mechanical repair met with raised eyebrows. And even the wine-tasting notes Lucky recited that evening didn't keep Helen from meeting Tyler at the kitchen door when he walked in a little after midnight.

"She was *what?*" Tyler rubbed his tired eyes and tried to concentrate on what Helen was saying.

"Up to her elbows in grease. She was fixing the sheriff's car. I saw it with my own two eyes. She's not setting an acceptable example for Bernadette. And you know what? Louise Cromwell has never even heard of a wealthy oilman named Dale Stinson. I tell you, Tyler, something doesn't add up with Miss Myers. And tonight…'' She rolled her eyes. ''Do you know what she wore to the table? White shoes. Not winter white, or cream or eggshell, but *white*, and it's long past Labor Day.''

''By all means, let's cut off her head.''

''I'm serious. This is not the sort of woman who should be instructing my granddaughter. You really should send Bernadette back to Houston with me. She's dying to go home—''

''She said that?''

''Not in so many words, but she did say she missed going to the theater with me and playing tennis and shopping, and I don't blame her one bit. You're always off doing whatever, rounding up God knows what while she sits in this house, isolated with a woman who doesn't know her white from her eggshell—''

''I'll talk to Miss Myers.'' When Helen didn't look satisfied, he added, ''And I'll think about Smithston.''

''That's all I'm asking.''

If only she knew how much she was really asking. Tyler would sooner go head-to-head with an angry bull than see Bernadette caught between two people she loved. Had his daughter really missed theater and tennis and shopping?

Granted, she'd been behaving more like Helen and less like her old self for the past few days, but he'd thought it was her contribution to their charade. An act. But maybe…

God knew he'd been dead wrong before. Last night, for example.

A *virgin*, and all along he'd thought Lucky's wide eyes, pouty lips and perfect body—so damned awkward and sexy at the same time—had all been a facade, her I've-never-been-kissed behavior a well-rehearsed act. But there was nothing rehearsed about Lucky, and that was the trouble. She was all too real. No fronts, no airs put on just for his benefit. She felt the chemistry between them and she didn't hide her reaction to him and her. The two of them. Together.

Whoa, son. Back up. There was no together. So they'd had sex? Sex was just sex, even if it was with a virgin. Especially since it was with *this* virgin.

Used-to-be-virgin. He shook off the guilt. She'd made her choice, and he'd made her no promises. He hadn't even hinted at the *C*-word. Hell, he hadn't thought past the lust clouding his brain. He'd needed to touch her, taste her, smell her, and then he had and it had felt so...right.

What the hell was he thinking?

What happened between them was completely, totally, irrevocably *wrong*. She was a tough-talking, gum-chewing cab-driver from Houston. Not the sort of woman who should be raising his daughter.

Hey—who said anything about raising Bennie? Lucky was temporary. One more week and she'd be gone. One week... His libido sent a wave of images to taunt him. Boy, what he could do with her in one week—

Last night was a mistake he wouldn't repeat no matter how much he wanted to. There was no future beyond her pretend nannyship. No happily-ever-after, with Helen breathing down his neck and the ranch weighing on his shoulders. He had too many problems and no answers. And Lucky definitely fit into the first category.

He needed a shower, a cup of coffee and a good kick in the butt, in no particular order.

"Daddy?" Bennie walked into the kitchen wearing a pink nightgown.

He did a double take. "A nightgown? What happened to your Simpsons T-shirt?"

"That's old news, Daddy. Grandmother brought me this. You like it?"

"It's..." Pink. "Pretty. Real pretty, honey."

Bennie smiled. "I knew you'd like it. Grandmother said Mama used to wear one just like it when she was my age."

Her hair was tousled, her features pale. She yawned and rubbed her eyes. "Are you okay?"

"Fine, honey." He rolled his head on his shoulders and sat down in a kitchen chair. She crawled into his lap and he rested his head on top of her soft hair. The smell of powder, soap and little girl sent a wave of affection through him and he hugged her. "I'm just tired."

"Me, too." She stifled another yawn.

"Late night?"

She nodded. "I was picking out my clothes for tomorrow. Grandmother and I are having brunch. Everybody who's anybody has brunch. Anyway, it was a toss-up between the yellow lace or the peach silk. The yellow's fine, but the peach brings out my complexion, don't you think?" Without waiting for a reply, she kissed his cheek and climbed from his lap. "Get some sleep, Daddy." Then she padded back to her room.

Picking out clothes? His I'd-rather-be-wearing-yesterday's-jeans daughter? And *brunch?*

He pinched his leg to make sure he wasn't having a nightmare. Ouch! So much for wishful thinking. He was stuck in reality with frilly pink nightgowns and peach silk brunch clothes and a mother-in-law who made Cinderella's wicked stepmom look like Parent of the Year. And worst of all, he was stuck with a woman—yes, a woman now—he couldn't have.

Forget reality. He was in hell.

TYLER FOUND Lucky bright and early the next morning near the garage, leaning under the hood of a '64 pink El Dorado Cadillac, Earline's pride and joy.

"I'm sorry to put you out like this, Lucky," the beautician drawled, "but that no good Jess Mangrum is as drunk as a skunk and I'm afraid this thing is gonna up and quit on me if I don't find out what all that noise is about. Billy said you sure were handy under the hood, so I thought what the hell?"

"No problem." Lucky emerged from under the hood, a

black fan belt dangling from her hands. "You need a new belt. I'll tighten this one as best I can until you can get a new one."

"You're a honey, that's what you are. Tyler's lucky he found you. I hope he plans to keep you around for a while."

"Not at this rate," Tyler said as he came up beside Earline.

Lucky jumped. "Geez, you scared me."

"Apparently not enough." He narrowed his gaze. "What are you doing out here?"

"Just finishing up." She slammed the hood shut and wiped her hands. "It's all yours, Earline. It should last you at least a couple of days, enough time to get a new one."

"Thanks so much. You're wonderful. She's wonderful," Earline added, turning to Tyler. "A real—"

"—honey, I know," he finished for her.

"I thought I told you to behave," Tyler said once Earline and her pink Cadillac had left. "You call playing town mechanic when you're supposed to be a refined nanny behaving?"

"Helen saw me," Lucky declared, guilt in her eyes.

He nodded and watched her chew on her bottom lip. The sight did nothing to feed his anger and everything to stoke the fire spreading to certain parts of his body.

"I was afraid of that," she said.

"Dammit, Lucky, why didn't you let Hank fix his own car?"

"Because he couldn't. Not all men are mechanically inclined, you know. Gender doesn't predispose you to certain interests. The battery connectors were corroded and I cleaned them. I was just being nice."

He reached out and wiped a smudge of oil from her cheek. "Don't be so nice next time. I need you to look and act like a lady for the next few days. Just until Saturday. Then Helen leaves."

"I didn't get a speck of dirt on my blouse," she quickly told him, motioning to the spotless cream silk she now wore.

He smiled, drinking in her impeccable appearance. "I have to hand it to you. No one would be able to tell you'd just been fixing someone's fan belt—" The words stalled in his throat as he glanced down at her shoes, one black and one navy.

"Geez," she said, her gaze following the direction of his. "I could have sworn those shoes were both the same color. Must've been the bad lighting."

"Bad lighting?"

"I already told you I'm not much of a morning person. I can't see clearly before 8:00 a.m. and I've been up since seven. So shoot me."

"Don't tempt me." He turned to stalk toward the Jeep. "Helen came at me last night with her guns blazing, so don't give her any more ammo."

"Wait—" She followed and grabbed his arm before he could climb into the Jeep.

"I've got fences to fix," he said.

"But I need to talk to you."

Here it comes, he thought. She wants to talk about the other night. To get into his head, pick his brain on everything from his feelings, to what china pattern he'd like. Damn, couldn't women get it through their heads that sex was just sex sometimes? Did they always have to talk everything to death?

"Hank had some news about your runaway nanny."

Whew, that was close.

"Thanks for telling me," he said after she repeated everything Smokey had told her. "I'll go into town later today and ID the pictures."

"Good." She started to turn away. "Happy fence-fixing."

"Lucky, wait. I... About the other night." *Hey, who was that?* Oh, God, it was him. He shook his head. Stop that. "You have to understand that it was just..."

"A mistake?"

"I was thinking temporary insanity, but mistake works, too."

"That's what I thought you'd say."

"And you agree?"

She smiled. "Fat chance, Tyler Grant. I've been waiting my whole adult life for what happened the other night, and I won't let your guilt mess this up for me. I'm basking."

"Basking?"

"And glowing, so stop feeling guilty."

"I took your virginity. How am I supposed to feel?"

"You didn't *take* anything. I gave it to you, buddy. My choice. You don't owe me anything. So stop worrying about me slipping a noose around your neck."

And just what did she have against slipping a noose around his neck? He was an attractive guy. A good catch. Only he didn't want to be caught. He was already caught between a rock and a hard place with Helen and the ranch and life in general.

"Stop beating yourself up," she told him. "Just forget it."

"I don't want to forget it. I *have* to. Can you understand that? No, I guess you can't. You were close to your dad. But me…" He shook his head. "I could kick myself now for tagging along after my mother and leaving my father. I try to picture how I'd feel if Bennie up and left me for Helen. It would kill me."

"You were just a kid then and Bennie would never do that."

"No, because I won't see her backed into a corner. I want to stay here with my dad, and that means keeping Helen happy, and that means giving Bennie every opportunity to be the lady her mother was. She can have that right here in Ulysses. She *can*."

She touched his arm, her fingers warm and soothing. "She does. She's learning tons of stuff, and I think she's even starting to like it. I don't have to nag to get her to put on a dress or do her studies, and she hasn't burped or snorted tea through her nose not once. She's even mastered Beethoven's Fifth on the piano, and she's a whiz at conjugating French verbs."

He gave her an incredulous look. "French? *Bennie?*"

"*Mais oui, mon cher.* Bennie taught me. I can say it in Italian, too. Want to hear?"

But he'd heard enough. *My beloved.*

He smiled. Then frowned. Then he kissed her.

11

IT WAS A KISS straight out of a steamy romance novel. Lots of clutching and grasping. Plenty of panting and moaning. Heaving chests and racing hearts. And then it was over.

"I—I guess that was a mistake, too," she said, gasping for a breath as Tyler staggered backward a few feet.

"Yes." His eyes were dark and desperate, riveted on her parted lips. "No... Hell, I don't know."

"We could try it again. Then maybe you could make up your mind."

He stared at her long and hard before he grinned. "I don't think that would be a good idea."

"Why's that?"

"Because I'd have you spread-eagle on the front of this Jeep, making an even bigger mistake than a kiss."

Speaking of bigger... Her gaze dropped to the prominent bulge in his jeans and her eyes widened. "Did I...do that?"

"Damn, woman," he growled, his gaze going to the sky. "What did I do to deserve this? Kick a cat in a past life?"

Her eyes narrowed. "I just asked a simple question. You don't have to fly off the handle."

"Simple? *Simple?*" He glared at her. "Do you know what those simple questions, those simple, wide-eyed, innocent questions do to me? They turn me on, that's what. Hell, Lucky. I'm only human."

"I really turn you on?"

He threw up his hands. "I give up. I'd better go before..."

"Before..." Her gaze went to the front of the Jeep and her cheeks heated.

"*Before*," he growled, sliding behind the wheel.

"YOUR RADIATOR'S busted," Lucky declared the next day as she stared through a thick layer of steam at Doris, Earline's assistant. "I can patch it up, but you'll have to replace it."

"Can't you replace it?"

Lucky smiled. "I'm fresh out of radiators, but any gas station should be able to order one."

"There's only one station in town, and that's Jess Mangrum's place. The man's three sheets to the wind most of the time. That's why, when Earline said what a great mechanic you were, I raced right out here."

Lucky patched the radiator while Bennie stood lookout. Tyler's new shipment of cattle had kept him away from the house most of the day, and Helen had moved on from hiring a band to redesigning the promotional materials to reflect the changes she'd been forced to make. At the moment she was poring over typestyles and various layouts, but Lucky wasn't taking any chances.

Guilt shot through her and she forced it aside. It wasn't as if she was breaking her promise to Tyler. Of the cars she'd fixed, not one of them had had a faulty belt.

"Thanks so much," Doris said, handing Lucky a box of homemade pralines. "Just a token of my appreciation."

"Can you teach me how to fix a car?" Bennie asked later as she and Lucky munched on warm pralines.

"Your daddy would have my hide. Fixing cars isn't very ladylike."

"What about fixing tractors?" Bennie asked when they walked around to the front of the house.

Lucky came up short, her gaze fixed on the green monster sitting in the driveway, a very frantic-looking teenager perched in the driver's seat. The teenager turned out to be Johnny

Simmons, the oldest son of a neighboring rancher. "It's hard to steer and the lift doesn't work," he told her.

"This is way out of my league. It's a *tractor*."

"Come on, Miss Lucky. Earline told Charlotte Webster who told Billy Jenkins, whose little brother is in 4-H with my kid brother, that you fixed her Cadillac. *And* Bud Shiney's Buick and Ray Michaels's Impala and…"

"But I don't know beans about tractors."

"They're just like cars," Bennie said, surveying the tractor. "That's what Jed says."

Lucky peered inside. "Well, it's got a steering wheel, but there's no gas pedal. That's not like a car."

"You don't have to drive it," Johnny said. "Just fix it. Please, Miss Lucky." He sounded so desperate, and Lucky was a sucker for desperate.

Ten minutes later, they'd pushed the tractor behind the garage. Lucky went to work under the hood while a nervous Johnny went inside for a piece of Mabel's pie.

It wasn't too far off from a normal car engine, but it had a hydraulics system unlike anything Lucky had ever seen. She spent a good half hour studying Jed's tractor for comparison.

"I think the hydraulic lines were crossed," she finally determined. "It looks like the lift line was going to the steering, and vice versa." For the next hour, she unfastened the connectors and reran the lines.

"Let's try it out," Bennie said once Lucky had finished.

"No." Lucky wiped her hands on a rag.

"Come on, Lucky." A mischievous light glittered in Bennie's eye. "How will you know it works if you don't start her up?"

Lucky shook her head and walked over to her cab. "Johnny can do it." She leaned into the trunk. "Bennie, can you hand me that wrench—" Her words drowned in the roar of a tractor.

She jerked up, her head banging the trunk lid. "Ouch—" The word caught as she swiveled around and saw Bennie sitting in the driver's seat of the tractor. "Bennie, get down from there."

"Let's take a little ride. Come on, Lucky." She gunned the engine. "It'll be fun—oops!" Bennie's foot slid off the clutch and the tractor lurched forward.

"Bennie!" The tractor jerked and launched across the backyard, headed out to pasture. Lucky bolted after it. She ran beside the tractor, grabbed the edge of the seat and tried to pull herself up. "Turn it off!"

"I can't. I—" Bennie wrestled with the steering wheel. The tractor made a sharp right and nearly took Lucky's arm out of its socket. "Lucky! Help me. I can't stop it!"

The back door burst open and Mabel rushed through. "What the sweet Jesus is going on? Oh no! Bennie, Lucky! Hold on. I'll get some help."

Hold on. Was she kidding? Lucky fought for a grip and barely managed to pull herself onto the seat of the speeding tractor. "Over," she shouted above the engine's roar as she grabbed hold of the steering wheel.

"Let up on the gas!" Bennie screamed from the seat beside her. "Hurry eeeeeeeeee!" Bennie jerked at Lucky's sleeve. "Watch where you're going—" They rolled over a stretch of barbed-wire fence, across the pasture toward a small duck pond.

"Come back here, dadblasted city gal!" Lucky twisted to see Ulysses dart off the back porch in hot pursuit *without* his shotgun. There was a God—

"Lucky, watch it!" Bennie screamed and Lucky swung back in time to see the edge of the duck pond. She swerved, and found out that big bulky tractors didn't actually swerve. She fumbled with the brakes, and lurched to a stop just as the tractor plunged into the water. She and Bennie pitched forward, straight over the nose of the machine, into the murky pond.

"You gals all right?" Ulysses asked when he and Mabel reached the pond.

Lucky spit out a mouthful of water and gasped for air as she struggled to her feet. *Ugh.* She plucked a lily pad from her dripping hair and trudged around the submerged tractor, her pumps sinking two inches with each step.

"That was great!" Bennie followed her, not the least bit upset that she was soaking wet and covered with some kind of slimy green weed. "Mega cool, wasn't it, Lucky?"

"Cool?" Lucky took a deep breath and tried to calm her pounding heart. Water trickled down her face and she wiped her stinging eyes with the edge of her sleeve. "You almost got us *killed,* Bennie. I could be duck food right now—"

"You're responsible for this, Bernadette?"

Lucky's eyes snapped open to find Helen in front of them. "I didn't mean to—"

"To get caught on the tractor with me," Lucky cut in. "But I needed her to show me how to start this baby up." She patted the tractor's rear bumper. "Then my foot slipped and off we went."

"You." Helen turned her narrowed gaze away from her granddaughter and the look of relief on Bennie's face was almost enough to ease the dread churning in Lucky's stomach. If only Helen hadn't been steaming as bad as the half-submerged tractor.

"Now, now," Ulysses said. "Let the girl be."

Wait a second. Ulysses taking up for her? Maybe she'd hit her head during the dive into the pond. Maybe she was even dead.

"It was an accident," he went on and Lucky pinched herself. Pain radiated up to her head. Definitely alive. Unfortunately. "It's over. No harm done."

"An accident? You call my granddaughter trapped on a runaway tractor and thrown into a nasty swamp an *accident?* It's a disaster, a travesty. A shameful display of adult supervision. You can bet Tyler's going to hear about this, and you, Miss Myers, will be looking for a new job."

And Lucky had no doubt that it was true. Driving a tractor

into a pond was sure to classify as a breach of her promise to Tyler. Even though she was fairly certain the tractor didn't even have a fan belt.

IT WASN'T HELEN who met Tyler at the door when he returned that evening. It was his father.

"Is Helen mad?" Tyler asked after he'd heard the story.

"Are you kidding, boy? She'd be waiting here right now, 'cept Mabel gave her something for her migraine. A little of Jed's moonshine. Told her it was medicinal tea." He chuckled. "Best medicine around. She's been sleepin' like a baby for the past hour, and she's sure to be out all night. Look, boy, I know this puts you in a bind, but don't be too hard on Lucky."

"She was fixing cars and tractors when I told her not to."

"She was helpin' folks out, and the tractor wreck was an accident." When Tyler shot him a look, Ulysses cleared his throat. "Uh, not that I seen it, mind, but Mabel relayed every detail."

"Do you mind telling me what brought on all the sympathy for Lucky? I thought you didn't like her."

"Never said that."

"Not in so many words, but you nearly shot her the first day, and you've been griping about her ever since."

"She ain't so bad."

"She's got a big mouth," Tyler said.

"The gal speaks her mind. Cain't fault her for that."

"She's stubborn."

"Just standin' up for herself. 'Sides, she's mighty handy with her toolbox." He chuckled. "She even fixed my old projector." When Tyler's gaze narrowed again, Ulysses added, "Not that I'll be watching any movies in the near future, not with my dadburned eyes being out of commission. Still, it's the thought that counts. Nice gal."

Later, as Tyler showered and changed, he thought over his father's sudden about-face. His father had always been a fair man, but since the breakup with Tyler's mother, he hadn't

taken kindly to outsiders, especially females. He'd been hostile
to all of Bernadette's nannies because he feared one of them
would steal his son away. But Tyler wasn't going anywhere.
He was staying until Ulysses made a complete recovery, and
so was Bernadette, and Lucky was going to behave herself.
Or else.

A HALF HOUR LATER, Tyler found her sitting on the front seat
of her cab, her toolbox beside her.

"My dad gave me this for my sixteenth birthday." She
touched the worn red metal. "I really miss him."

Something softened inside him, and he stiffened. He was
mad, he reminded himself. Mad and out for blood. "Is that
why you put a tractor in the duck pond? A tractor you
shouldn't have been fixing in the first place?"

"Okay, get it over with," she said, closing her eyes.

"You promised me, Lucky."

"I know, and I broke my promise, though I didn't really
break it, not technically. I didn't fix any fan belts. But I did
work on a few cars, though Helen didn't see me. She only
saw the tractor, so did your dad and Mabel. I figured he'd be
getting the rope ready for Helen to string me up."

"Dad's stubborn and can be mean when he wants to be,
but you fixed his projector. That old thing means a lot to him.
He would have staged a standoff with the whole damned town
on your behalf."

"He did seem excited when I showed it to him." She
grinned. "He actually opened the glass case and let me touch
the esteemed cowboy hat and boots. Boy, your father really
liked James Dean."

"My father *was* James Dean. That was the trouble. My
mother wanted a Rock Hudson and she got James Dean. A
Jett Rink instead of a Bick Benedict. My parents met for the
first time at the premiere of *Giant* at the Austin Palladium.
My father had just finished working his way through Texas
A&M, as an agricultural science major, and my mother had

just returned from a boarding school in London. They met during intermission.

"She had romantic notions about huge cattle ranches and lots of money," he went on. "My father had a ranch, all right, but only a few acres and a small shack right here where this house is. He'd just bought the land and was barely starting out. The reality of ranch life didn't quite meet her expectations, and neither did my father, but it was too late by then. They were already married, and she was already pregnant with me, and divorce wasn't an option as far as her parents were concerned." He shook his head. "It didn't work. My mother was used to lots of money, servants, city life. My father worked hard for her, built this place up, but it wasn't enough. Her parents died in a car accident, she inherited the family money and left when I was sixteen, and I went with her."

"But why? You seem like you love it here."

"I do. I did. But I also loved my mother and I wanted her to love me. I thought if I acted the way she wanted, became the man she'd wanted my father to be, it would make a difference." He shook his head. "The only thing it did was break my father's heart. He lost his faith when we left, sold off pieces of the ranch and let the herd dwindle." Determination swept his features. "But I'm changing all that." He felt her hand on his arm and warmth spread through him.

"No wonder you don't share your father's love for those old movies."

"They're all reminders, *Giant* in particular, of a time in my life I'd rather forget. I remember my parents fighting. My mom would retreat to her bedroom and my dad would hole up in the library, watching his movies, wishing for a happy ending like the one on screen. It always made me sad to see him like that."

"Where is your mother now?"

"Living in Connecticut, recently remarried to some Wall Street wizard. She's happy, I suppose. We don't talk much."

"Her loss," Lucky said, and pleasure spiked through him. "I'm sorry I messed things up. Was Helen really mad?"

"I don't know yet. She's sleeping. I expect she'll be fit to be tied."

She sat there for a long moment, her gaze fixed straight ahead. "She thinks she's better than me," Lucky finally said. "She thinks she's better than everyone."

Lucky shook her head. "I grew up in a small place, went to public school. My clothes were clean, but worn." She continued to stare off into the distance. "But I never felt second best. I had my parents and I knew they loved me. You know," she went on, "my happiest memory is of one Thanksgiving we spent in my father's cab. He had to work, otherwise we weren't going to eat that month, and instead of sulking at home, my mother packed up the turkey and the dressing, bundled me up, and we ate dinner in the parking lot of O'Hare Airport." She smiled. "It was cold and cramped, but I've never felt as warm in my entire life."

"You're a lot luckier than you think, Lucky Myers." He lifted his hand, his fingertips going to her mouth. Her lips were soft. They parted beneath the slight pressure of his touch. Soft, and warm, and so damned tempting. *No!* If he kissed her once, he would want to do it again, and again, and then...

"Are you up for a little sight-seeing?" he asked.

"Are you kidding? I'm going stir-crazy. Give me five minutes."

When they met back outside near Tyler's Jeep, Lucky had traded in her worn tennis shoes for a pair of shiny red boots.

"Where in the world did you get those?"

She looked pleased. "From my fix-it stash. I've got a box of homemade pecan pralines, a recipe book and a coupon for a free manicure at Earline's."

"It seems you're getting pretty popular around here." He climbed in next to her and gunned the engine. He caught her sideways glance and saw the grin tugging at her lips.

"What can I say? I give great transmission."

"THIS IS LIKE a bad episode of 'Hee-Haw.'" She stared at the smoke-filled interior of Billy Ray's, Grant County's only and most notorious honky-tonk.

"I know it's a bit down to earth…" A crowd of people filled the place, despite the fact that it was only Tuesday night. Longnecks in hand, they whooped and hollered, a fast country two-step blaring from the sound system.

"It's not that. I don't feel above it." She drank in the dozens of women wearing western shirts, jeans and belt buckles big enough to eat dinner off of. "I just feel different," she added. Her gaze collided with his. "Out of place."

He reached for the hem of her T-shirt and knotted it at her waist. His knuckles skimmed her midriff and electricity sizzled across her skin. "You look casual and country. Perfect."

"Tyler!" They both turned to see Hank. "Got some news on your nanny. Even with the ID you made on her, she slipped past them New York cops and made it into Canada where she scammed a wealthy Canadian. Now they're as hot to catch her as we are."

"Keep me posted," Tyler said after turning down Smokey's offer of a beer.

"Lucky! Hey, Lucky!" Earline's excited voice carried from a table set up near the entrance.

"What are you doing?" Lucky asked, her gaze taking in the stack of applications and mountain of neon pink fliers.

"Signing up Hickory Honey wannabes for this year's pageant. It's Friday, you know. You will be at the festival, won't you?" Earline poked a finger at Tyler. "She can't miss the festival. I'm crowning this year's Honeys."

"She'll be there," Tyler promised. The next song started and he tugged her toward the dance floor. "Let's dance."

"Okay, but if I step on your toes, it's your own fault."

"I'm liable to be the one stepping on your toes. I haven't done this in a long time. Too long," he added in a regretful voice and Lucky squeezed his hand and gave him a dazzling smile.

He swung her into his arms, and then she was laughing and smiling and doing her best to follow his lead. She missed a few steps, but even that was fun. There was the encouragement of all the couples that sailed past, and by the time Lucky collapsed on her seat, she could hardly breathe, her face hurt from smiling, and warmth bubbled inside her.

"I think you're a hit," he said. "You must have been busy the past few days. How many cars did you fix?"

"Altogether about ten." She shot him a worried glance. "I already said I was sorry."

"Say it tomorrow. I'm not mad tonight."

She smiled and sipped the soda he'd ordered for her. "Then I'll take advantage of your good mood."

"Now that sounds interesting."

"I wish it would get interesting," she whispered to herself, her heart beating faster. "Much more interesting."

AN HOUR LATER, they left Billy Ray's, hand in hand, and headed for the ranch. A quiet silence engulfed them as he parked the Jeep out back and they simply sat there, staring up at the stars.

"It's always like this out here," he told her. "I used to walk out onto the balcony of my apartment in Houston, but even on the clearest night, you couldn't see this many stars."

"It's beautiful."

"Yes," he said, but he wasn't looking above them. He was looking at her. "You really have a great mouth."

"Nobody's ever said that to me before. I've heard I have a big mouth, a smart mouth, a loud mouth, but—"

Warm fingertips pressed against her lips. "All of the above, too. But I was talking more about the shape of your mouth. Perfect for kissing." His lips closed over hers for a long, delicious moment.

"You did it again," she said when their lips finally parted. "You said you weren't going to kiss me and here you are—"

"I'm not." He pulled her closer. "I can't."

"I know. It would never work." She slid her arms around his neck. "Never."

"Ever," he added, then he kissed her again, his mouth fierce and desperate now, as if he'd been away from her far too long.

Eager hands slipped under the hem of her T-shirt to caress her bare skin. Electricity danced along her nerve endings, sending sparks to her nipples, her thighs. Then his mouth left hers to kiss a wicked path down her neck, and lower, until his hot breath warmed the fabric covering her nipple.

"You're not wearing a bra." His voice was ragged.

"No one usually notices."

"I noticed."

She opened her mouth, but the only sound that escaped was a loud gasp as his wet mouth closed over the stiff peak. She clutched at his shoulders, pulling him closer, closer—

"Hell's bells, Tyler! Do you know what time it is?"

Ulysses's voice echoed in her ears and they both jerked upright, like two teenagers caught in the back seat of a car. Or the front seat of a wide-open Jeep. The spell was broken. "Saved by the bell," Tyler muttered.

Bell? Damn but these Grant men had an obsession with bells.

12

"SHE ENDANGERED Bernadette's life," Helen exclaimed the next morning. "That sort of behavior is intolerable."

"It was an accident," Tyler said.

"She's supposed to be teaching Bernadette how to be a lady, Tyler. Not how to change spark plugs or fix transmissions. That's why the world has mechanics."

"So Miss Myers has a few eccentric hobbies. You enjoy needlepoint and playing bridge."

"I hardly see a comparison."

Neither did he, but he was desperate, and he hadn't become the Grant in Landry, Preston and Grant Investments by letting someone outwit or outtalk him. He could play hardball with the best, and Helen ranked up there in the top ten.

"Of course there's a comparison," he went on. "You're good at needlepoint and bridge. Extremely good," he added, watching Helen's face soften. "Which is one reason you enjoy both activities. Miss Myers happens to be more mechanically inclined, and so her leisurely pursuits are geared more in that direction—"

"Sorry to interrupt you, son, but there's a phone call for Helen." Ulysses appeared in the doorway, cordless phone in hand. "You two-timing Merle, woman?"

"I'm sure it's Julius Morrow, the photographer for the *Houston Star*. They've agreed to do a cover promotion for the museum benefit and they want to come out here to get a few preliminary photos. This isn't exactly the sort of image I had in mind, but Julius assured me that the rustic look is in right now. He'll be here Friday morning." She took the phone. "Julius, dear, how are you?"

Tyler didn't wait for her to finish her call. He had work to do, and while Helen wasn't completely satisfied, she was busy and that would keep her focused on her own affairs rather than on Lucky for a little while longer.

Long enough for this entire fiasco to be finished. Four days, Tyler told himself. She'd already fixed a number of cars and waterlogged a runaway tractor. What else could happen?

"YOU WANT ME to *what?*"

"Enter the Hickory Honey competition with me," Bennie said. "Come on, Lucky. I'll be in the junior division, and you'll be in the senior. We'll prove to Grandmother that we're real ladies. She loves pageants. She's a huge supporter of Miss Picasso and Miss Merlot, oh, and Miss Delphi, too."

"Run those by me again."

"Miss Picasso—the most talented new female artist in Texas. And there's Miss Merlot, the best female wine connoisseur. Miss Delphi is the title for the most cultured debutante in Houston."

"I think this is a little different, honey." Visions of Earline ran through Lucky's head. Boobs out to there, big Texas hair up to here, blue eye shadow bright enough to land an airplane in a thick fog. "Don't you think the Hickory Honey competition is a little more...down-to-earth than your grandmother's used to?"

"Granddaddy said it's the fanciest shindig this side of Dallas." Great. A shindig to impress Helen. Not!

"It's perfect," Bennie said enthusiastically. "You have to do this with me, Lucky. I'd be too embarrassed by myself, but with you, I know I could work up the nerve. We'll get all dressed up and walk around in high heels. Grandmother will love it. She'll forget all about the tractor thing." She grabbed Lucky's hand. "Please, please, *please.*"

No. It was there on the tip of her tongue. Just say no.

"Please," Bennie added, and Lucky nodded. *Wimp.*

"This is great." Bennie jumped around. "You're great. Just wait until Grandmother sees us. She'll be speechless."

Helen speechless? This might not be so bad after all.

"STELLA, it's me. How's my granny?"

"Fine. The boys have taken a real liking to her. Can't say as I blame them. She's so sweet."

A warmth spread through Lucky. "If she asks, tell her I'll be home soon. So how did we do against the Munson Cab Magpies?"

"We forfeited, and I never was so glad. I thought bowling would be fun, but I can't seem to get into the game."

"They had to forfeit because you didn't want to play?"

"Oh, no. The guys had other plans."

"What could be more important than bowling and beer?"

"Your granny invited everybody to her bingo game. It was great. I won fifty bucks, and Buster won a hundred. He even met a new girl. The bingo caller. Gladys, I think her name was."

Granny was fine, the guys weren't mad and Buster had a new babe. All was right with the world. Now if only Lucky could see things turn out as good right here in Ulysses. Fat chance. She was headed for blue eye shadow and teased hair, and the worst night of her life. Just her luck.

"I NEED A FAVOR," Lucky told Tyler Thursday morning when she finally managed to work up enough nerve to talk to him about the beauty pageant. Sort of.

"Me, too." Bennie waltzed in on Lucky's heels. "It's very, very important, and you absolutely *have* to do it, otherwise, our plan will be ruined and Grandmother will stay mad and—"

"Okay," Tyler agreed before she could go on. "As long as it's not painful or illegal."

"It's not illegal," Lucky assured him. "But I'm not so sure

about the painful part.'' He shot her a questioning gaze, and she added, ''We want you to keep Helen busy tomorrow while Bennie and I go into town for the day. We'll meet you and Helen at the high school tomorrow night for the festival kick-off.''

''All day?''

She grinned. ''So it's painful. You're a strong guy.''

''Please, Daddy.'' Bennie threw her arms around his waist.

Tyler smiled, then the expression faded into a sniff. ''Bernadette, are you wearing perfume?''

Bennie smiled up at him. ''Grandmother gave it to me. Smells good, huh? It was Mom's favorite.''

''And what's on your cheeks?''

Bennie beamed. ''Pale Pink Parfait. Grandmother said Mom wore perfume and blush when she was my age, and lip gloss, too, but I keep chewing that off. So what do you think?''

''It's…nice, honey. Though you might lighten up a little.'' He shot a glance at Lucky that said, *Is she old enough for this stuff?*

Lucky shrugged. *Look who you're asking.*

''So promise you'll help us surprise Grandmother?'' Bennie said.

''What's the surprise?''

''If I told you, it wouldn't be a surprise. Just have Grandmother there by seven.''

''I'll try, but I don't think she'll go.'' He looked into his daughter's face, so full of hope, and sighed. ''Helen's going to have a fit if you're not here tomorrow. Some photographer is driving in from Houston to take publicity photos for her fund-raiser.''

''That's even more perfect,'' Bennie declared. ''You have to get her to the festival, Daddy. It'll be a prime photo opportunity. Please, please, *please.*''

Oh no. Bennie was doing the please thing again. Maybe Tyler wouldn't be as marshmallow soft as she was. Maybe he would put a stop to things before… The big sucker.

"Thank you, Daddy. Thank you, thank you, *thank you.*" Bennie gave him another hug then darted out of the library.

"Hey," he said when Lucky started to follow. "Aren't you going to thank me, too?"

"For signing my death certificate?"

He frowned and motioned her into a chair in front of him. "What are you talking about?"

She sank into soft leather and shook her head. "Nothing. Listen, thanks. This means a lot to Bennie."

"Yeah." He slumped on the corner of the desk and Lucky had the overwhelming urge to reach up and touch his shadowed jaw. He was so beautiful and brooding and...celibate.

Not that it wasn't his own fault. She was ready and willing and able and...in love.

As if that mattered. She was in love with a man she couldn't have. One who wouldn't have her. Forget unlucky. She was cursed. What next? A swarm of locusts?

"She's growing up so fast, I can't keep up. Perfume, of all things. And that Peppermint Pink Popsicle stuff."

"That's Pale Pink Parfait."

"Yeah, that, too." He shook his head. "She's nearly a teenager and I'm clueless as to what to do with her. For her. About her."

Lucky gripped the arms of the chair. She wasn't going to touch him. Not for all the croissants in France. All the mufflers at Muffler Mania. No way. Uh-uh.

Hair-sprinkled muscle met the warmth of her palm. "Just love her, Tyler." She stroked his forearm. "That's all she really needs from you. Just love." *Bad hand.* Down, girl. Down. She managed to pry her hand away from him.

Okay, distance was better. No touching. She glared at her hand. You got that? Do that again and your history, sister.

"I wish things were that simple." He shook his head. "Bennie needs more, things I can't give her. She needs a woman to show her all this pink pickle stuff."

"You're off by an entire food group," Lucky muttered.

"It's *parfait*, not pickle. One's dairy and the other's vegetable, and whoever heard of a pink pickle anyway?"

"See?" He threw up his hands. "I'm totally clueless. Nan did all the woman things with Bennie. When she died, I thought I could step in. Bennie had always been so much like me—wild and unruly. Since she was knee-high, she loved to wrestle and watch sports. She could spit farther than any toddler I'd ever seen."

"You must have been proud."

He beamed. "I'm always proud of her." His face fell. "But now I don't know what to do. She's growing up and she's turning into a woman." He stared at Lucky. "She needs a woman."

"I think you're the one who needs a woman." *Who said that?* Okay, so she had, but it wasn't as if she could help herself. He was standing right there in front of her, his denim-clad family jewels at eye level, about to pop a zipper. So she'd looked, and she'd commented. Big deal? At least she hadn't touched.

Why hadn't she touched?

"I do," he growled. "And I'm in a helluva mess because of it." He stalked behind the desk, his *big deal* disappearing behind several inches of thick mahogany.

"Because why?"

"Because I want you."

"Me? You really want—"

"Don't even start. I have enough to worry about right now. Let's just try to make it through the next couple of days without touching or kissing, or doing anything really stupid. Okay?"

So kissing her was stupid? Yes. It was because it wouldn't stop there and it had to because there was no future for them. She knew that, yet it didn't ease the knot in her chest or dispel the urge to slap his handsome, stupid face.

"And you think your father's the blind one?" She bolted to her feet and glared at him. "You know something, Tyler?

You are clueless. You're the most clueless man I've ever met. You give new meaning to the word." She turned and left him staring after her. *And the only really stupid thing I ever did was fall in love with you.*

LOVE WAS A BITCH. Lucky spent Thursday night tossing and turning, plotting ways to kill Tyler. Painful ways. Of course, she would always stop just short of actually doing him in, but the moments leading up to her change of heart were pretty good. Lots of crying and begging on his part. Still, her wimping out prevented any real satisfaction and she awoke grouchy and puffy and thoroughly unhappy.

As luck would have it, Lucky didn't even have the satisfaction of wallowing in her own misery. Bennie hauled her out of bed before the crack of dawn to get an early start into town. Mabel drove them in Jed's pickup, the bed full of her cooking entries: pecan pie, pecan cake, butter-pecan syrup, pecan pralines, pecan divinity and candied pecans.

"Lucky!" Earline squealed, intercepting her as she climbed out of the truck outside the high-school gymnasium where the festival was being held. Hooking her arm through Lucky's, Earline steered her two pageant hopefuls toward her pink Cadillac.

"We've got a ton of things to do before—oh, no, sugar." Earline frowned as she studied Lucky's face. "You're full of water. Oh, well," she brightened and started the ignition. "No need to worry. I know a surefire trick. We'll wrap you in cling wrap and sit you out in the sun for a few hours."

"Isn't that dangerous?"

"Only if you stay out too long. But we'll bring you in and unwrap you well before you dehydrate. You don't have a thing to worry about. I swear you won't end up like Sara Mae Mulberry."

"She dehydrated?"

Earline nodded. "And suffered sunstroke. She was so out of it, she stood up at the annual church picnic and did a striptease when the choir sang 'Beulah Land.'" At Lucky's horrified expression, the woman added, "But that was before I perfected the wrap." She patted Lucky's arm. "No need to worry. You're in good hands, sugar, and the choir's not even doing 'Beulah Land' tonight."

"WE'RE HERE," Earline declared late that afternoon when they reached the gym. She cast a pride-filled glance at Lucky and Bennie. "I'm telling you, it's in the bag."

Lucky took a deep breath, glanced down at the dress Earline had spent most of the afternoon altering, a red sequined number that hugged every minute curve, minus the excess water, of course. It was a bit more revealing than she was used to. Used to? Okay, so she had underwear that left more to the imagination than Earline's *lucky* dress, as the woman had called it.

But Lucky needed some luck. Especially tonight.

Bennie, on the other hand, had an angel sitting on her shoulder. Beautiful in a pink dress and pink pumps and a matching shade of pale pink lipstick, she was a shoe-in to win. Lucky smiled. Maybe this would work.

"WHAT IN HEAVEN'S NAME is going on?" Helen followed Tyler into the crowded gymnasium, all the while voicing the same complaint she'd made not five minutes ago in the truck, then before that on the way to town, then back at the house. "We're wasting Julius's time traipsing all over the place, chasing after Bernadette. All we need are some simple shots."

"You'll get them," Tyler promised. "Now, let's find a seat."

"In here?" Her gaze swept the already overflowing rows of bleachers. "You have to be kidding. There's no back to these chairs. Everyone is all crammed together. Dreadful," she huffed. "Simply dreadful."

"Positively," Julius, long blond hair pulled back in a chic ponytail, quickly agreed. "And the lighting is hideous."

"Oh, hush up, the two of you," Ulysses grumbled. "I cain't concentrate with all that cackling."

"For your information," Helen said, bristling, "I don't cackle."

"Cackle, cackle," Ulysses grumbled.

"Oh, shut up, you heathen."

"Uptight old biddy—"

"Hey, Tyler!" Hank called to him from a few rows away, effectively drowning out Ulysses's insult. "Good news. We got her! Canadian government nabbed her before she caught a plane to France. Recovered a load of stuff, too, you lucky son of a gun!"

"What is that man bellowing about?" Helen demanded, squeezing after Tyler down a crowded bleacher.

"Nothing."

"It didn't seem like nothing. Who was nabbed?"

"Yes, who?" Julius asked. "It sounds positively scandalous."

"Mind your own business," Ulysses said. "A man cain't even have a moment's peace with the two of you yacking."

"I don't yack."

"Yack, yack—"

"Quiet," Tyler said, sliding into a vacant spot and pulling Helen after him. "It's showtime."

"GOOD EVENING, folks! Welcome to the fourteenth annual Hickory Honey competition. I'm your hostess with the mostess, Earline Butterworth, and here's our first contestant."

Five contestants trailed by before Earline's assistant grabbed Lucky's elbow and herded her up to her mark.

"You're next," Doris said. "When Earline says your name, start walking."

Lucky nodded and rubbed her damp palms together. *You can do this.* For Bennie. You can walk through fire, dance over hot coals, bake in cling wrap like a leftover piece of chicken...

"Our next contestant is new to Ulysses... Let's give a great big welcome to Lucky Myers!"

Lucky took a deep breath, stared straight ahead and strolled onto the walkway. Strolled, not stumbled, even though she was wearing three-inch heels. All those lessons had paid off. She smiled. This wasn't so bad. Just a few more feet, a little turn, and she'd be finished.

She hit the end of the runway and paused. Helen stared back from the second row, her eyes filled with shock. Panic bolted through Lucky and she stumbled. Then she saw Tyler. The way he looked at her, his blue eyes filled with so much—wonder, appreciation, hunger.

She caught her balance, pushed her shoulders back and smiled even wider. She turned, slowly and gracefully, hips swaying. *Eat your heart out, Tyler Grant,* and sashayed back up the runway to a round of cheers and applause.

"One down," she said, rushing backstage to stand next to Bennie who hugged her excitedly.

"You looked great! Did Grandmother see you? Oh, she must have died. I bet she apologizes for every mean thing she's ever said to you. Oh, this is great!"

"Come on, Bennie." Doris motioned the girl forward.

"Knock 'em dead," Lucky said, crossing her fingers. Helen in particular.

"And in our junior division, we have Ulysses's own Miss Bernadette Grant..."

Bernadette walked out onto the runway, her steps practiced and careful, and pride surged through Lucky. Bennie looked so beautiful. So ladylike. So sweet—

"Whoa!" Bennie squealed, arms flailing as she caught her heel on her hem and fell backward. She landed on her rump and slid out onto the runway, like a lacy pink bowling ball aiming for the center pin.

"What in heaven's name—" Helen's shout echoed above the background music. She gestured wildly toward the stage, then to the man next to her who clicked picture after picture with an expensive-looking camera. Uh-oh. Lucky winced as Helen grabbed the camera and yanked the man around like a French poodle on a leash. Take that, Jacques. And that. And that, you camera-snapping, ponytail-wearing Frenchie.

It was too painful. She couldn't watch. Her gaze shifted to Tyler who'd bolted to his feet to plow over the first two rows of people to get to his daughter. But Bennie was already scrambling to her feet. She dusted herself off and tossed a grin at her father. Tyler stopped, one leg hooked over the seat.

"Now for my next trick," she declared. "A quadruple backward flip." She kicked off her pumps and made her way back up the stage in a perfect succession of flips.

The audience went wild. Lucky joined in, applauding and cheering before her gaze found Tyler again. Her hands went limp.

He was still straddling the seats, to the dismay of the people in front of him. Not that he cared. He had this silly, dreamy look on his face, a smile tilting his lips, pride brightening his eyes. Something twisted in Lucky's gut and she all but melted into a red-sequined puddle.

Geez, she had it bad.

And that wasn't good.

"I was terrible." Bennie giggled, then moaned and threw herself into Lucky's arms.

"You were wonderful!"

"I fell and Grandmother had a coronary." Breathlessly, Bennie peered around the stage curtains. "She's still having a coronary." Bennie frowned and caught her lip between her teeth as she surveyed Helen and Frenchie. "I guess I really messed things up this time." Her head drooped and she stared at her now-shoeless feet. "I'm sorry, Lucky."

"Don't be sorry! This whole thing was a great idea, and it would've worked. It still might..."

Bennie shook her head. "You don't have to make me feel better. This is a disaster. This never would have happened to my mama. She was so pretty and graceful. She did everything

right, said the right things, wore the right clothes.'' The girl
turned eyes bright with tears on Lucky. "But me... I'll never
be half as good as she was, and Daddy will never love me
half as much.''

"Oh, Bennie.'' Lucky hugged the girl tight. "That's not
true. Your father loves you.''

"Not enough,'' Bennie cried into Lucky's shoulder. "I'm
not enough. I've read all the right books and watched those
instructional videos you found in Dad's library. I want to be
a lady like my mama. More than I've ever wanted anything.''

"It's all right,'' Lucky crooned. "Come on, baby. They're
about to announce the winners. Let's go get you some tissues.''

TYLER WATCHED as Lucky hustled Bennie toward the ladies'
room. His daughter's voice echoed in his ears. *I want to be a
lady...*

So it hadn't been an act. The interest in clothes, Beethoven's
Fifth, all those French verbs... She really did want to learn all
that stuff, to be the lady her mother had been.

And she didn't stand a chance of doing it stuck way out
here in Ulysses, with books and videos. To be like Nan, she
needed the same opportunities—Smithston and Houston and
Helen. *Damn.*

"There you are!'' *Speak of the devil.* Tyler turned to face
Helen. "This is all your fault,'' his mother-in-law said. "Julius
is headed for the nearest FedEx office right now to overnight
those horrible pictures back to Houston for tomorrow's society
column.''

"I'm sorry.''

"I know you're dead set on staying here in this god-awful
place,'' she said. "But I really wish you would open your
eyes and smell the cappuccino, Tyler— What did you say?''

"I said I'm sorry.'' He raked a hand through his hair. "For
bringing you and Julius here tonight. It was a mistake. Bringing Bennie to Ulysses was a mistake.''

"Of course it was. This dreadful place is completely and totally unacceptable. Houston is her home. For heaven's sake, Tyler, she should be with other young ladies her age, not out risking her life on runaway tractors and pageant runways, and with that...that nanny."

"I know."

"You should fire that woman immediately— What did you say?"

"Dammit, Helen. Don't make this any harder on me. I said you were right. Houston is her home. I... Dammit."

"Are you saying you're letting me take her back?"

"I'm saying I'm taking her back."

"Thank God." Helen threw her hands up in the air. "You've finally come to your senses." She beamed. "Things will be absolutely perfect. Ulysses is all wrong for you, Tyler. You don't belong here."

But he did, he thought as he watched Helen disappear back into the gymnasium and found himself caught up amid a crowd of well-wishers backstage.

"Great kid you got there, Tyler. A regular chip off the old block. It's so good to have you back. You planning on joining the singles group over at the church? We'd love to have you come in and talk to the 4-H group at the school. I hear you're planning on increasing the herd? Bet your daddy's real happy about that. Proud, too."

This was the one and only place he'd ever really belonged, and sixteen years ago he'd walked away of his own free will and made the worst mistake of his life. He couldn't do it again, yet he couldn't say goodbye to his daughter. He wouldn't do that. He and Bennie belonged together, and they would stay together, even if it meant giving up the ranch for Houston. He'd walk through hell for her and challenge the devil to a fistfight.

And he'd break an old man's heart. Again.

Yep, he'd definitely done something terrible in a past life.

Forget kicking the cat. He'd probably run over the damned thing.

"GIVE ME that blasted gun, girlie. I've got a snooty battle-ax of a mother-in-law to get rid of." Ulysses grabbed the gun, aimed at the colored balloons and started firing.

Pop. Pop-pop. Pop. Pop-pop-pop-pop-pop—

"Dad!" Tyler walked up to the balloon booth and yanked the imitation Uzi out of his father's hands. "What are you doing?"

"Killin' me a woman, son."

"He's won two purple stuffed teddy bears and a polka-dot alligator." The girl at the booth stacked Ulysses's prizes on the counter.

"Damn straight. How many till I get that hot-pink turtle?"

"Five in a row."

"Take that, Smellin' Helen." Ulysses grabbed another gun from the counter and started firing again.

"Dad."

"Don't bother me now, boy. I'm concentratin'." *Pop. Pop.*

"Your aim's really good."

"Thank you, boy. Now quiet." *Pop-pop. Pop-pop-pop.*

"Especially considering you're blind."

Pop! The gun went limp in Ulysses's hands and he threw his arms up in the air. "It's a miracle, son. I've been healed. Praise be!"

"Dad." Tyler tapped him on the shoulder.

"Don't bother me now, son. I'm givin' thanks to the Lord."

"You've been able to see since the bandages came off, haven't you?"

"I know I'm a sinner, Lord. But now I aim to change my ways. Thank you for smilin' on me and givin' me my eyes back."

"You've been lying to me."

"And forgive my boy here for doubtin' your blessings."

"That time in the barn with Lucky. You walked in front of

her on purpose and she covered for you. She knew, too, right?''

"I'll be in church every Sunday mornin' from here till the day I meet my maker.''

"Mabel was in on it, too. And Jed.''

Ulysses turned two angry red eyes on Tyler. "Don't be taintin' Mabel's name like that. She's a good woman.''

"So you fooled her, too?''

"Shame on you for doubtin' the Lord's work.'' Ulysses turned his arms up at the sky again. "I won't be slippin' any more quarters out of the offerin' ever again.''

"Shame on you, Dad.''

"Aw, hell, boy.'' Ulysses let his arms drop.

"Why, Dad?''

"You came home, boy, and I wanted you and Bennie to stay permanently. I thought if you thought I needed you—''

"That we'd stay.''

Ulysses nodded. "I know it was a low trick—and Mabel had no part of it, mind you. The woman's a saint. But I did what I had to. I didn't want to let you go again.''

"I'm sorry, Dad. Sorry I left, sorry I hurt you, sorry the ranch suffered because of it.''

"Now, that's the last thing you ought to be sorry for. The ranch is just land.''

"But you worked hard for it.''

"Not for *it*, boy, for your ma. For you. All I ever wanted was a little piece of land, a few head of cattle. I'm a simple man, Tyler. Always have been. Your ma didn't understand that. I built this place up for her. When she left, it lost its meaning.'' He shook his head. "Now I ain't blamin' things on her. She's a good woman, she's just different from me, is all. She wanted different things out of life. I loved her and wanted her happy, so I let her go. I let you go, too, because I wanted you to be happy. And I'll let you go now if it's what you want.''

"I want Bennie to be happy.''

"Then do what you have to, boy. Your old daddy understands."

It was as if a weight had been lifted. Tyler took a deep breath and for the first time he didn't feel the tightness in his chest. The guilt. "Thanks, Dad."

"Don't worry none about me," Ulysses went on. "I'll be fine. Why, my hearing's nearly shot, but it ought to last a good six months more. And if I decide to have that surgery on my old arthritic knees, why, I'm sure I won't be laid up more 'n a few months. Three or four at the most. Mabel and Jed can run things, even if the ranch is a good size larger thanks to you. But don't go frettin' over us. We'll manage—"

"Dad."

"Oh, go on." Ulysses waved him away. "I've got a hot-pink turtle to win for my grandbaby. A going-away present." He slapped a twenty on the counter. "Maybe I'll even get something for Lucky." He picked up the Uzi and aimed. "Take that Yellin' Helen, you old nosy, highfalutin, pain-in-the-ass, hemorroid-causin' nanny goat..."

The words faded in a string of *pops* as Tyler headed back inside the gym. He still had a loose end to tie up, one that belonged to a beautiful and lethal-to-his-sanity cabdriver.

And for the first time since he'd decided to return to Houston, Tyler actually smiled.

13

"CONGRATULATIONS, Lucky! You deserve it, darlin'! Glad to have you here in Ulysses, sugar! Hey, Lucky, I've got this knocking in my engine…"

The praises and well-wishes surrounded Lucky as she shook hands, accepted hugs and smiled so much her cheeks felt ready to explode. This beauty-pageant business was tough stuff, especially since Lucky had never in her wildest dreams expected to win. She'd hadn't even wanted to win. But winning felt kind of nice, especially for the invisible flat-chested woman.

"I knew you could do it!" Earline hugged Lucky. "This lucky dress has never let me down. It was made for a winner!"

If only Lucky's prize were a hunky cowboy instead of a new saddle and a year's supply of hoof-and-nail cream. But as usual, Lady Luck wasn't shining on her, she realized when Bennie rushed up to her and told her she'd just talked to Ulysses who said he'd just talked to Tyler who'd said he'd just talked to Helen. Bennie and Tyler were going back to Houston.

"It's all my fault!" Bennie started to cry again. "I fell and now Grandmother is mad, and so is Daddy, and this is my punishment for entering the stupid beauty pageant in the first place. How could I have had such a crazy idea?"

"You didn't. I did."

Bennie shook her head. "You can't take the blame again. And it won't matter anyway. It's settled. We're going back and that means you're not going to be my nanny anymore and I was really hoping you would end up staying and—"

"That's not in the cards, baby." Lucky wiped the moisture from Bennie's cheek. "I was only temporary. You know that."

"This isn't fair," Bennie wailed. "It's not supposed to turn out like this. We're friends."

"And we'll always be friends, no matter how far apart we are, or if your father hires a dozen more nannies. You'll always be special to me and I'm really going to miss you." Bennie threw her arms around her and the tears Lucky had been fighting spilled over. "You're really special," Lucky whispered. "Always remember that. You're special and beautiful and..." *I love you, and I love your dad, and I love it here.* But she couldn't say any of those things. It would only make leaving more difficult. "I—I'm going to catch a ride with Earline," Lucky said instead, putting Bennie away from her. She dashed the wetness away and tried to gather her control.

"Don't cry," Bennie said.

"I'm not. I—I just have something in my eye." Lucky hurried away as fast as three-inch heels and a skintight straight dress allowed. She was going to save Tyler the trouble of firing her and leave tonight.

She already had a portion of her money. She could leave Tyler a note with an address where to send the rest. He would make good on his deal, she knew that, though she wouldn't blame him if he changed his mind, especially when he realized Lucky was responsible for tonight. Her letter would spell everything out. *My idea. I'm the uncultured ditz. The harebrained schemer.* No way would she let Bennie take the rap. Lucky could still see the shock on Helen's face that brief moment when they'd made eye contact. There'd be hell to pay for tonight.

She pushed her way through the crowd backstage in search of Earline.

Chicken, a voice whispered.

So? Better to be a chicken and leave before she made a fool of herself and cried in front of Tyler Grant.

Tough-as-nails Lucky Myers didn't cry. Crying was for sissies. Or babies. Or lonely women hopelessly in love for the first time in their life.

And Lucky didn't qualify, she told herself. She didn't.

SHE WAS LEAVING.

He'd known it when he'd found her missing from the festival. But somehow it hadn't seemed quite real. Now, as he stood at the open garage door and watched her fumble with her car keys, reality hit him like a fist in the gut.

"Darn it." She tried unsuccessfully to unlock the door of her cab.

"Sneaking off without saying goodbye?"

"Saving you the hassle of firing me." She tried the key again and missed by a good inch. "Just for the record, I didn't try to mess things up on purpose. I really thought Helen would be pleased when she saw Bennie looking so pretty and lady-like." She sniffled.

"Are you crying?"

She shook her head and swiped at her nose with a raggedy tissue. "Of course not."

"You are." He stepped forward, the knowledge drawing him, touching something deep inside him that he'd tried so hard to bury. "You're crying."

"You must have been by the homemade-wine booth." She sniffled again. "You're imagining things. I never cry." She yanked open the car door.

"We need to talk, Lucky."

"Look, I didn't mean to make things worse for you," she said. "I wanted to make up for the tractor incident. I had no idea Helen would go ballistic when she saw Bennie—"

"Not about tonight. About you. Me...us."

"*Us?* Since when is there an us?"

"Since...since I took your—accepted your virginity. Now

there's an us. A me. A you... By the way, you looked great tonight. You deserved to win.''

"Thanks to you. You taught me that getting dressed up can be fun. But it's not me, Tyler. Some pretty clothes and a lot of makeup can't change who I am."

"Please don't cry."

"I'm *not* crying."

"It's okay. It's healthy. Women cry all the time."

"Look," she said, turning wide, bright eyes on him. The first of the festival's fireworks sizzled across the night sky in brilliant jags of blue and purple and red. Shadows played across her damp face, making her look vulnerable, despite her murderous gaze. "For the record, crying has nothing to do with being a woman. I can belch, cuss and spit with the best of them, you included, Tyler Grant, and don't you forget it." She climbed in and moved to close her door, but his hand blocked the way. "Now move it or lose it, buddy. I've got things to do."

"We're not through. We—"

"There is no we. You said yourself it would never work between us. I'm a tough-talking, gum-chewing cabdriver from the wrong side of the tracks. Hardly your type."

"Dammit, woman, you don't know what my type is."

"So tell me." Lucky gave him a pointed stare. A burst of green stars overhead revealed the wetness on her cheeks.

"You," he said truthfully. "You. A woman who's real. One who isn't afraid to butt heads with me. One who tells the truth and makes my daughter laugh. A woman who turns me inside out, and turns me on."

"*Used* to turn you on. The novelty wore off right after I gave and you accepted." The flood of multicolored Roman candle dazzle spilled past the open garage door. "You went slumming for a little while, and now it's back to country-club living—women with legs up to here, breasts out to there, designer clothes and a family name you can trace clear back to the prehistoric era—your type, buddy. Face it, Tyler. You want everything I'm not."

He laughed, a harsh, angry sound that stirred his blood as fiercely as her words. "With the way I'm feeling now, I'd definitely argue that. And for the record, your legs are pretty damned long. And pretty damned *pretty*." He grabbed her arm and in two strides pulled her to the door of the garage. Then he hauled her flush against him. "And I want you, Lucky. I miss you." Before she knew what was happening, he lifted her onto the trunk of the Chevy and pushed her dress clear up to her thighs.

"This doesn't solve anything," she murmured as his lips ate at hers. "I mean, it does solve one thing, but not the important things." She tugged at his shirt while he worked the zipper of her dress. "Not that you, uh, your...well, you know, isn't important. It is, and I want you and I—"

"Damn, but you talk too much, woman."

"Did you say woman?"

"Uh-huh."

She smiled. "That's what I thought you said." Then she met his lips in a bone-melting kiss that ended with her flat on her back, sprawled on the Chevy's trunk, fireworks bursting overhead. "I'm still not your type."

"Yeah, yeah. No breasts out to here." He pushed down the bodice of her dress and closed his hungry mouth over one nipple. He nibbled and suckled while she gasped and panted. "Or legs up to there." His hand traveled her leg, pushing material up until his fingers reached the silk-covered heat between her thighs.

"And the name," she murmured. "Don't forget the name."

He pulled away from her, staring deep into her eyes as he slid panties and panty hose down her legs and pulled them free. "*Lucky.* Your name is Lucky. I don't care about tracing it, or impressing people with it. I'm the only one that need to be impressed." He glanced down at his straining denim. "And I'm pretty damned impressed right now." He ripped hi shirt up and off, then worked at his jeans. The deft slide of fingers, the hiss of a zipper and he was ready. "You do this to me, Lucky."

"Any woman would do that. You're a normal, hot-blooded male. You automatically get aroused. I could be anyone." Even as she said the words, she heard the challenge in them. The eagerness for him to prove her wrong, to make her feel special. To make her feel like a desirable woman, for once in her life. Okay, so make that twice.

"No one makes me this crazy." He stroked his rigid length and desire spiraled through her. "No one makes me ache this much, burn this hot. Just you." She heard the conviction in his voice, saw the sincerity in his eyes, and warmth filled her.

A warmth that had nothing to do with the sexual tension gripping her body and everything to do with the undeniable fact that she loved this man. She *loved* him.

"You really want me that much—" He silenced the question with an urgent kiss.

"Don't even think about doing that right now," he said when he ended the kiss. "I'm ready to explode, and if you start all those innocent, breathy questions, I'm liable to explode right here and now, and I thought we'd go for someplace a little more private."

But the thought of him pulling away from her for even a few seconds was unbearable. She needed to touch him. To feel him. Her hands skimmed his shoulders, clutched at his muscles. "This is private."

"We're on top of a car." He kissed her long and hard.

"But everyone's still at the festival."

"This is true."

"And I really need you right now."

"But we're outside."

"You're outside." She sucked in a ragged breath. "That's the problem. I need you inside. Now. *Please.*"

"You're the boss, honey." He pulled her to the edge of the car and plunged into her with one deft stroke.

She sighed and he groaned, his forehead against hers, eyes closed for a long moment. "I've needed this for so long," he murmured. "I've needed you for so long. I've been such a jerk."

"I'll say."

"I'm sorry, Lucky. I really am. Do you forgive me?" He stared down at her, so desperate and unsure and her heart went out to him.

She smiled. And gasped. "Move it or lose it, buddy. It's not nice to keep a lady waiting."

"Yes, ma'am." He kissed her long and slow and deep, while his erection throbbed inside her. Anticipation skittered along her nerve endings, priming them, readying them for the devastating assault of feeling that was sure to follow.

He didn't disappoint her. He cupped her buttocks, rocked her against him. Slow at first. Then his fingers flexed, muscles bunched and he urged her closer, himself deeper. He moved her faster, his hips bucking, hers rocking. Faster and harder. Deeper and more desperate. Then it came. The heavens opened up, trumpets blared and the angels sang.

Heat flooded her, washing through, melting her until she collapsed against Tyler's sweat-slick, heaving chest. He drove deep one last time, groaned and clutched her fiercely. As they held each other, hearts beating a frenzy, breaths shallow and fierce, the sky faded to a serene black.

"The fireworks are over," she finally said, the statement true in more ways than one. Everyone would be home soon. Reality check. "We'd better get dressed."

He lifted his head to stare at her. "I don't care whose type you think you are. You…me…we'll make this work out for us."

Joy rushed through her, his words capturing her heart the way his strong arms captured her body. He wanted her with him, despite who she was, because of who she was.

"Will you marry me?"

"I think that's my line," he said.

"Then I accept."

"I'm not asking." He shook his head and moved away from her. "Dammit, Lucky. I can't. I want to, I would in a heart-beat, but I can't."

A sad smile lifted her mouth. "That's what I thought you'd say." She righted her dress, retrieved her panties and started to pull them on. Tyler fastened his jeans and reached for his shirt.

"We'll hook up in Houston," he said. "And I'll set you up in an apartment close by me. A nice high-rise or some-thing."

She blinked back the sudden tears and tried to keep her voice steady. "I'm sorry, Tyler. It's all or nothing." What the hell was she saying? She loved him, she wanted him. So it wasn't marriage? It was the best offer anyone had made her in a long time. Try ever. So maybe he thought it wouldn't work now. The closer they became, the more hopelessly in love he fell, he'd start to see things her way. All she had to do was say yes.

"No. This would never work between us. I want what my parents had. Love. Endless, boundless, I'll-love-you-till-doomsday-and-beyond love."

Shrugging away, she started toward her cab. He caught her by the shoulders and forced her to face him. "I do love you."

"Not enough." She pulled away and surprisingly, he let her.

"Please, Lucky. Don't... I'll take care of your grand-mother." He said the words as if he was negotiating a business deal instead of the rest of her life. Gone was the sexy cowboy who smiled and flirted and made her feel good inside. In his place was a cold, calculating businessman who didn't take no for an answer. Suddenly she realized how different they were.

It had nothing to do with looks or money or sophistication. They were different because they valued different things.

Tyler valued money and what it could buy him.

And Lucky valued her self-respect.

"You won't ever have to worry about another nursing-home payment." He ticked off the advantages. "I'll take care of both of you. You can quit your cab driving and finish your degree at the University of Houston. I'm offering you money and stability, Lucky. Everything." *Nothing.*

She didn't say a word. There was nothing to say. She walked toward her cab, praying with each step that her pride would hold together what was left of her heart before she turned and raced back to his arms. She was crazy. She should be jumping for joy, thanking the heavens. *He loved her!*

"Dammit, Lucky!"

She slid behind the steering wheel and slammed the door.

"I want to give you more," he said, following her. He leaned into the window. "I do."

A sad smile curved her lips as she stared up at him. "You're going to miss me, Tyler Grant." And then she kissed him, a slow, savoring kiss that ripped at her heart. "I—I have to go," she said as a car turned into the other side of the double driveway. Headlights blazed, illuminating Tyler's dark, troubled face.

His gaze darkened as he touched her cheek, his thumb catching a trickle of wetness.

"Yes," she admitted softly. "I'm crying." Then she shoved the cab into reverse and left Tyler Grant staring after her.

"THAT WAS LUCKY," Mabel said, half a dozen blue ribbons pinned across the front of her blouse.

"She's really gone," Bennie whispered.

"It's about time," Helen added.

"Oh, pooh-pooh," Julius exclaimed. "I wanted more pictures."

"You all right, son?" Ulysses asked.

"No." He turned to stride out to the barn. He was lonely, heartbroken and mad as hell at himself. Good Lord, he'd offered to *buy* her. What had he been thinking?

He hadn't been thinking, he'd been feeling. Desperation had

closed in on him and he'd reacted the only way he knew how when it came to the people he loved.

He'd tried to buy his mother's acceptance by marrying into enough old money to put a sizable dent in the national deficit. He'd tried to buy his father's forgiveness by putting Reata back together. And he'd tried to buy Lucky's love by offering to care for her and her grandmother.

All last-ditch efforts. All failures.

Lucky couldn't be bought. Or changed. Or compromised.

He'd tried to do all three, but the funny thing was, he loved her even more because she'd refused him. She was Lucky.

And she'd left him.

"YOU MADE HER LEAVE!"

Bennie's angry voice drew Tyler down the darkened hallway to the library. He started to open the door, then he heard Helen.

"She shouldn't have been here in the first place, Bernadette. She's hardly qualified to care for you."

"She's more than qualified. She was my friend, Grandmother. My *friend*. How could you make Daddy fire her?"

"I didn't make your father do anything. He agrees with me and wants what's best for you. And I don't appreciate your tone of voice, Bernadette Willemina Bell."

"I'm a *Grant*," Bennie said. "I'm not a Bell. I never wanted to be one. I love you, but I won't ever be what you and Daddy want me to be. I'm different, and so is Lucky. But there's nothing wrong with that."

"I see the sooner you return to Houston, the better."

"I don't want to go," Bennie said, her chin rising a notch. "I like it here."

"But Smithston..."

"I never wanted to go to Smithston. I want to go to school in Ulysses." Her voice broke. "I know I'm not all the things you want me to be," Bennie went on. "But can't you love me anyway? I try to like the same things as you. That's why

I entered the beauty pageant. I wanted to please you and Daddy, to make you both proud of me.'' Bennie was crying full force.

Tyler didn't blame her. He felt like crying himself.

I won't ever be what you and Daddy want me to be. You and Daddy... *Daddy.* He pushed open the door and walked inside just as Helen wrapped her arms around Bennie.

''Oh, sweetheart, I am proud of you,'' Helen said, and for the first time, Tyler saw a tear roll down his mother-in-law's cheek. It stopped him dead in his tracks. ''I don't mean to make you feel awkward, dear,'' she went on. ''I simply want the best for you. Your father and I both do, that's why we're all going back to Houston—''

''We're not going,'' Tyler cut in. ''We're staying right here.'' He faced his daughter. ''You did all of this for me, didn't you? The piano lessons, the French, the dresses... You really have no interest in those things, do you?''

She stared guiltily at her feet and wiped her eyes. ''You're always telling me, 'Wear a dress, Bennie. Act like a lady.' I thought you wanted me to like all those things, to be like Mama.''

''Oh, baby.'' He pulled her into his arms. ''Your mother was your mother, and you're you. I don't care what you like as long as you're happy. That's all I ever wanted. I don't want you to feel torn between me and Helen, between our different ways of life. I want you to have everything you want.''

''But I already do.'' She stared up at him through glistening eyes. ''I have you and Granddaddy, Grandfather and Grandmother.'' Her gaze went to Helen. ''I love you, Grandmother, but I also love jeans and ratty sneakers and pet lizards. Maybe I won't like those things when I grow up. Maybe I'll like tea and museums and opera. Maybe not. But I want you to love me anyway.'' Her gaze lifted to Tyler's. ''I want you to love me.''

''I couldn't love you more, sweetheart.''

''Then bring Lucky back. I love her, and so do you.''

"What?" Helen's shocked voice drew both their gazes.

Tyler smiled down at his daughter and gave her a wink. "Can you excuse us, honey?" Bennie nodded and left the room, and Tyler turned to Helen. "Bennie and I are staying here. No more nannies, and Bernadette goes to school in town. You can fight me if you want to, but I'm asking you not to. For Bennie's sake."

"If I do, I'll lose her, won't I?"

"Yes, and I don't want that. You're her grandmother, Helen. You should be a part of her life."

For the first time, Tyler saw Helen's shoulders actually slump. She looked...vulnerable. He did a double take. Yeah, vulnerable. Who would've figured?

"I'm very headstrong, Tyler," she went on in a defeated voice. "I know that, it's just that I've always had to be. My father expected it of me and I couldn't let him down. My father was strict with me, he pushed me hard, always afraid I wouldn't fit in, that someone would realize a Bell wasn't so perfect."

"No child is perfect."

"His would have been. That's why I had to be. No one could know that the great Samuel Bell couldn't father a child." She stared up at him, a sad look on her face. "I'm adopted, Tyler. I know that doesn't make up for my pushiness, but perhaps it helps you understand a little better why I am the way I am. I had to live up to the Bell name, so no one would ever doubt that I was Samuel Bell's daughter, so he wouldn't doubt it."

"Nan never told me."

"She never knew. No one does. Just my parents and Merle, and now you." She wiped at a tear. A melancholy smile lit her eyes. "Nan always said I was a snob, and she was right." She closed her eyes. "I miss her so much." Her expression grew serious. "Do you really love this Lucky person?"

He nodded. "More than you can imagine."

"Well, then." She took a deep breath and wiped at her

tears. "You do what you have to do. Be happy, Tyler," she said, patting his shoulder. "And keep Bernadette happy. And this old snob will take herself home and butt out of your business."

"Praise be, it's about time." Ulysses stood in the doorway and munched a bowl of ice cream. "Two miracles in one night. That must be some kinda record, eh, son?"

"Dad," Tyler said in warning.

"Don't trouble yourself, Tyler," Helen said. "I can handle *that*." She jabbed a finger in Ulysses's direction and fire lit her eyes. "It'll be a pleasure to leave you behind. No, no, I take that back. It would be a pleasure to leave you six feet under."

Ulysses waggled his eyebrows. "Gettin' spunky on me, huh, Helen?"

"I am not and have never been spunky. Bold, yes. Self-assured, of course—"

"Stuck-up, and how!"

"Hateful man," she huffed.

"Ugly woman."

"Old billy goat."

"Snooty know-it-all."

"You two should get a room," Tyler said. His father hooted, Helen bristled, and Mabel appeared in the doorway with a broom. He left the three of them to their bickering and headed down the hall to pack. Now to set things right.

14

"LUCKY?" Stella's concerned voice came over the CB radio as Lucky sat, her engine idling, in the cabbie lane outside of Houston's Intercontinental Airport.

"I'm here, Stella. What do you need?"

"Just checking on you. Me and the boys have been worried about you the past two days since you got back. You have to snap out of this. How about bowling this weekend? We're playing the Burnin' Rubber Bald Eagles and they've got a new guy on their team. Young, single, cute. And I heard from Marge, the dispatcher at Burnin' Rubber, he's in the market for a wife. Perfect for you."

For the old Lucky. But she was different now. She'd given up her manhunting aspirations. She'd already found a man, caught him and turned him loose. She stunk at hunting.

"I'm really not up to meeting anyone right now."

"Come on, Lucky. You have to pick yourself up and get on with your life."

"I will," she promised. "Soon." But at the rate she was going, she'd be too heavy to pick herself up.

Yesterday alone, she'd consumed an entire quart of ice cream, half a dozen doughnuts and a chocolate-fudge cake Buster had brought over to the nursing home for her granny. While two days wasn't enough time to gain any real weight, she'd be fat and miserable in no time.

Right now she was just miserable.

All or nothing...

If only nothing didn't feel like...well, nothing.

The back door of her cab opened, shattering Lucky's thoughts. Thankfully. "Where to, mister?"

"An all-night wedding chapel."

"Excuse me?" Lucky pushed up the brim on her baseball cap and stared into her rearview mirror. A sly, devilish grin stared back at her and her heart kick-started before racing forward.

"I said, an all-night wedding chapel. I'm getting married. At least, I think I am." Tyler's voice was deep, rich and music to her ears. "I want you with me at Reata, as my wife. You can finish school, teach, fix cars, wreck tractors, do whatever you want, as long as you do it with me." He sat the familiar green lizard on the back of the seat between them. "And Marlon."

Her heart slammed against her ribs, threatening to burst free. *Calm, girl. Make sure he's for real.* She took a deep breath and stroked Marlon with her fingertip. His huge eyes closed and he sat there, lazy as ever. "What about Helen?"

"She's not marrying you. I am. At least, I hope I am."

"I mean, won't she have something to say about it?"

"Yeah. Congratulations." At her raised eyebrow, he added, "Okay, she'll say it grudgingly, but I don't care."

"I'm not a prime example of ladyhood. What about Bennie?"

"Bennie loves you, and she isn't the least bit interested in being a lady. It was all an act."

"I could have told you that."

"So why didn't you?"

"Would you have believed me?"

"Maybe." When she raised her eyebrow again, he added, "Okay, probably not. I told you, I'm only human. I've got faults. I'm stubborn and headstrong."

"And domineering and blind and infuriating and—"

"I get the picture. I'm all those things, and more. And I want you to marry me anyway. I know you covered for Bennie—the tractor thing, the beauty pageant—they were all her leas. She told me. That took a lot of guts to take Helen's wrath. I appreciate it, and I'm sorry."

"You're welcome, and don't be. I love Bennie."

"Then marry me and you can spend the rest of your life loving her." His voice took on a quiet note. "I want you, Lucky. More than I've ever wanted anything before. Marry me."

"I don't know." She chewed a fingernail and eyed him in the rearview mirror. "You're not exactly my type."

"And what is your type?"

You. But she wouldn't say that, not yet. Not after the pain, and extra calories he'd put her through.

"Well..." She turned on him, her knees on the front seat as she stared at him, dressed in faded jeans and a faded denim shirt. She quickly noted the dark shadow covering his jaw, the exhaustion carving his perfect features. Good. He looked every bit as bad as she felt. "Well, you're not exactly the kind of guy I'd take home to my granny."

He gave her a wicked grin. "Not enough of a gentleman?"

"Too much of a gentleman for someone like me. I don't know the first thing about what's in season or who the hottest designers are. My idea of a social event is an evening of bingo at the senior citizens' home. I don't know fine wine from Kool-Aid or a Monet from a Picasso. I wear white after Labor Day and I've never vacationed in the Hamptons or been mentioned in the society pages or—"

Two strong, warm fingers touched her lips, cutting her off. "I don't care about any of those things. I never did, I just got so caught up in making Helen happy I forgot that for a little while. It's not what's on the outside that counts—your clothes, your friends, your bank account. It's what's on the inside—a good heart, a kind and giving nature. I know what a real lady is, Lucky. Hell, I've always known. It's you." The words were quiet, *desperate,* and she couldn't refuse.

She dived over the back seat, straight into his arms, his life, this cowboy who made her feel wanted and wicked and ever, bit a lady for the first time in her life.

His lips captured hers and Lucky closed her eyes to th wonderful feeling. Heat skirted her senses, coaxing them t life. She felt the tickling on the inside of her thigh.

"Not now, Marlon." She giggled and squirmed. "Tyler' liable to get jealous…" She opened her eyes to see the lizar staring at her from his perch on the back of the seat.

"It's not Marlon this time." Tyler moved his fingers fo emphasis. "It's me."

She gasped and smiled. "He's been giving you lessons."

"I've been giving him lessons. So tell me," he said, hi lips hovering near hers, so close she felt the warm rush of hi breath. "Are we going to get lucky tonight?"

"You, cowboy, are going to get Lucky *every* night, an Marlon can find his own date."

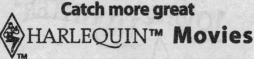

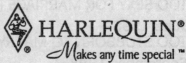

LOVE & LAUGHTER™

Marriage Makers

by
Cathie Linz

Once upon a time, three bumbling fairy god-mothers set out to find the Knight triplets their soul mates. But... Jason was too sexy, Ryan was too stubborn and Anastasia was just too smart to settle down.

But with the perfect match and a little fairy dust...
Happily Ever After is just a wish away!

March 1998—
TOO SEXY FOR MARRIAGE (#39)

June 1998—
TOO STUBBORN TO MARRY (#45)

September 1998—
TOO SMART FOR MARRIAGE (#51)

Available wherever Harlequin books are sold.

MEN at WORK

All work and no play?
Not these men!

July 1998

MACKENZIE'S LADY by Dallas Schulze

Undercover agent Mackenzie Donahue's
lazy smile and deep blue eyes were his best
weapons. But after rescuing—and kissing!—
damsel in distress Holly Reynolds, how could
he betray her by spying on her brother?

August 1998

MISS LIZ'S PASSION by Sherryl Woods

Todd Lewis could put up a building with ease,
but quailed at the sight of a classroom! Still,
Liz Gentry, his son's teacher, was no battle-ax,
and soon Todd started planning some
extracurricular activities of his own....

September 1998

A CLASSIC ENCOUNTER
by Emilie Richards

Doctor Chris Matthews was intelligent, sexy
and *very* good with his hands—which made
him all the more dangerous to single mom
Lizette St. Hilaire. So how long could she
resist Chris's special brand of TLC?

Available at your favorite retail outlet!

MEN AT WORK™

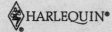 

Look us up on-line at: http://www.romance.net   PMAW2

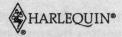

Not The Same Old Story!

 Exciting, glamorous romance stories that take readers around the world.

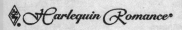 Sparkling, fresh and tender love stories that bring you pure romance.

 Bold and adventurous— Temptation is strong women, bad boys, great sex!

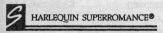 Provocative and realistic stories that celebrate life and love.

 Contemporary fairy tales—where anything is possible and where dreams come true.

 Heart-stopping, suspenseful adventures that combine the best of romance and mystery.

 Humorous and romantic stories that capture the lighter side of love.

Look us up on-line at: http://www.romance.net   HGENERIC

Don't miss these Harlequin favorites by some of our bestselling authors!